ALPHA BASE IS
THEIR BATTLEGROUND

DR. ANTHONY HARDING: The nuclear physicist was once an idealist who wanted to show the world right from wrong—but now his goals were money, power, and his own twisted glory . . .

VIKKI OSBORRN: She used all her feminine charms to help her team get inside Alpha Base. Now, with an innocent man's blood on her hands, there was no turning back . . .

COLONEL MACKLIN RENAULT: The mercenary knew that people killed for different reasons. His reason was simple, unsentimental, and very profitable . . .

MAJOR WILLIAM McGRIFFIN: As acting commander of Alpha Base, he missed the intoxicating freedom of flying jets. But recovering the hijacked nukes would be more exciting—and dangerous—than anything he'd ever known . . .

RAVES FOR DOUG BEASON'S
RETURN TO HONOR

"A military thriller of awesome proportions. . . . Experience this book!"

—Patrick Lucien Price, editor, *Amazing Stories*®

"Doug Beason's chilling scenario could well be tomorrow's shocking realism. . . . A gripping tale of military professionals doing what they do best: fight!"

—M. E. Morris, author of *Alpha Bug* and *The Icemen*

Books by Doug Beason

Assault on Alpha Base
Return to Honor

Published by POCKET BOOKS

ASSAULT ON ALPHA BASE

DOUG BEASON

POCKET BOOKS

New York   London   Toronto   Sydney   Tokyo   Singapore

This novel is a work of fiction. Names, characters, places, and incidents are either the product of the author's imagination or used fictitiously. Any resemblance to actual events, locales, organizations or persons, living or dead, is entirely coincidental and beyond the intent of either the author or publisher. The opinions expressed herein, explicit or implied, are purely those of the author and do not reflect the views of the United States, the Department of Defense, or the United States Air Force.

The author has never been involved in or had access to, either officially or unofficially, any aspect of nuclear weapons storage, security, transportation or safeguards. This novel is based on pure speculation, gleaned from material assimilated from *Aviation Week and Space Technology* and the books *U.S. Nuclear Warhead Production*, Vol 2, by T. Cochran, *et al*; *Nuclear Terrorism*, by Leventhal and Alexander; and *Preventing Nuclear Terrorism*, also by Leventhal and Alexander.

An *Original* Publication of POCKET BOOKS

 POCKET BOOKS, a division of Simon & Schuster Inc.
1230 Avenue of the Americas, New York, NY 10020

ISBN 978-1-4767-9716-8

First Pocket Books printing November 1990

10 9 8 7 6 5 4 3 2 1

POCKET and colophon are registered trademarks of Simon & Schuster Inc.

Printed in the U.S.A.

To Captain Jerry Allison, USAF Academy Class of 1976—friend and fighter pilot extraordinaire: *his untimely death at REDFLAG was our nation's loss.*

Acknowledgments

To: Dr. Clifford E. Rhoades, Jr., for the idea for this novel; Kevin J. Anderson, Michael Berch, Esq., Alan R. Gould, Colonel "Moose" Millard, Major Dave Harris, and the 1550th Combat Crew Training Wing for their detailed help and suggestions; my agent, Richard Curtis; and to my editor, Eric Tobias, for his patience and insight in making this book what it is.

Language of the Air Force

AAFES—Army Air Force Exchange Service (see BX)
AGL—Above Ground Level
APC—Armored Personnel Carrier
APU—Auxiliary Power Unit
AUTODIN—AUTOmatic DIgital Network
AUTOVON—AUTOmatic VOice Network
BASE OPS—Base Operations
BDU—Battle Dress Uniform (camouflaged fatigues)
BG—Brigadier General
BX—Base eXchange
CINCSAC—Comander IN Chief, Strategic Air Command
CMSGT—Chief Master Sergeant
COMM—communications
CP—Command Post
DNA—Defense Nuclear Agency
DOD—Department of Defense
DO—Director of Operations (Operations Officer)

Dooley—a freshman at the USAF Academy (translated as "slave" from Greek)

ECM—Electronic Counter Measures

ETA—Estimated Time of Arrival

FAC—Forward Air Controller

Firstie—a senior, or First Classman at the USAF Academy

Full Bull—Colonel

GUARD—Emergency radio frequency

Hole in the Ground—Snack bar on Wendover AFB

IFF—Identification Friend or Foe

IG—Inspector General

INF—Intermediate Nuclear Forces

IR—Infrared

IRST—Infrared Search and Track

JP-4—high-grade jet fuel

MAC—Military Air Command

MPC—Military Personnel Command

NCOIC—Non-Commissioned Officer In Charge

NEST—Nuclear Emergency Search Team

NTS—Nevada Test Site

Nonrated—a support officer, a nonflyer

NOTAM—NOtes To AirMen

NSA—National Security Agency

O'Club—Officer's Club

OD—Officer of the Day

OER—Officer Efficiency Report

OI—Operating Instructions

OJT—On the Job Training

ORI—Operational Readiness Inspection

PALS—Permissive Action Links (Anti-Nuclear Theft Devices)

PME—Professional Military Education

POST Stinger—anti-aircraft missile using Passive Optical Sensing Technology

POW—Prisoner of War

RAIDS—Radar Airborne Intrusion Detection System
Rated—a pilot or navigator, a flyer
ROTC—Reserve Officer Training Corps
RON—Remain Over Night
SAC—Strategic Air Command
SAP—Security police
Sky Cop—a SAP
Sixpack—a six passenger truck
SOP—Standard Operating Procedure
TAC—Tactical Air Command
Twixt—to send a teletype copy
TDY—Temporary DutY
Touri—slang for tourist
VFR—Visual Flight Rules
USAFA—United States Air Force Academy

On the strength of one link in the cable
Dependeth the might of the chain:
Who knows when thou mayest be tested?
So live that thou bearest the strain.

Ronald Arthur Hopwood
The Laws of the Navy, **Stanza 5**

Prologue

Alpha Base: an auxiliary base located five miles due west of Wendover Air Force Base, Utah

Dusk, and 102 degrees in the shade. As the sun set behind craggy mountains, the clouds ignited in a candy cotton pink. Inside of an hour the desert air would plummet thirty degrees. A chill would set in, washing across the crater, driving cold-blooded reptiles to their lairs.

A set of four razor-wire fences, spaced twenty yards apart, ran in front of the Bronco. Airman First Class George Britnell sat in the truck, just inside the fourth fence. Separated by meticulously cleared sand, the fences symbolized all that Britnell hated about the Air Force: strict, confining, and mindless. Every fifty feet on the fences blue-bordered white signs screamed in red lettering:

1

WARNING!
This installation is
OFF LIMITS
to all personnel!
Use of deadly force authorized
by order of the Installation Commander

The warning was repeated in Spanish.

Britnell drew in a lungful of smoke. Another minute and the light would be gone. The infrared detectors embedded along the fence would be able to detect even the innocuous glow from his cigarette.

The day shift was almost too easy—if he wanted to screw off, it was a simple matter of driving out here to the opposite side of Alpha Base, away from the gates and people. No one was stupid enough to approach the complex during the day. With the signs and warnings, you would have to be blind to come near. Even the animals had a sixth sense about the inside fence. You didn't have to read to tell that the faint hum and smell of ozone yammered 120,000 volts of electricity.

Airman First Class Lucius Clayborn, Britnell's partner, threw a glance at Britnell. "You about done, man?"

Britnell took a final hit. He stepped from the Bronco and ground the cigarette with his heel. "Yeah." He pulled himself up and slammed the door.

The truck lurched off and found pavement. They headed around the meteor crater that held Alpha Base, following the fences. Britnell unrolled his window. The smell of sage washed in, mixing with the sparse juniper and piñon pine covering the back side of the crater.

Below the crater's lip concrete bunkers dotted the depression. Twenty feet wide and twelve feet high, the

2

bunkers were set into the side of the half-mile-deep cavity. Searchlights squatted on top of each bunker, their glass covered by levered metal shutters. Yellow warning signs adorned the bunkers. The red international symbol for radioactive material was stenciled on each sign.

Row after row, clustered in groups of three and four, the bunkers covered the five-mile-diameter basin. Britnell had once counted over three hundred bunkers before stopping. Wendover AFB was to the east; Britnell could make out the shimmer of runway lights on the main base.

Clayborn pulled the Bronco off the road. White dust swirled around them. "It's been a while since we checked in. Do you want to make contact?"

"Yeah, I'll make the call." Britnell fumbled for the microphone. "Apple One, this is Busyfly validating our position. Our location is"—Britnell squinted at the marker set by the road—"Foxtrot Two Zero—I repeat, Foxtrot Two Zero."

A moment passed. "I copy, Busyfly. Disengage your IFF now."

Britnell reached under the radio and toggled the Identification Friend or Foe system, turning the device off, then back on. Originally developed so that Air Force fighters could distinguish between friendly and enemy planes, this fifth-generation IFF sent out a coded signal that directed the radar to ignore its presence; when the IFF was turned on, the radar and warning systems on Alpha Base would electronically mask the jeep's presence from detection.

"I copy your position, Busyfly."

"Roger that." Britnell clicked off the mike and grinned. They continued around Alpha Base—

The truck lit up in a fireball of light and sirens. Searchlights punched through the dusk, bathing the

1

Earlier the same day: Wednesday, 1 June, 0730 local

Wendover Air Force Base, Utah

Major William McGriffin stopped before the command post. Set into the door, a one-way mirror reflected the major's image back to him. His blue eyes inspected his hair. He liked to keep his hair thick on the sides and long in back, but he had just plastered the locks down in anticipation of meeting his new boss, the Wendover base commander. He was pushing the weight limit for his height, but all cargo pilots seemed to be slightly pudgy. It was the twenty-hour flights to exotic places like Diego Garcia, Pusan, and Thule that gave him his padded frame.

But there were not going to be any more exotic places for McGriffin, at least for a while. He had just about accepted being yanked off his flying job and forced to work at Wendover AFB. Wendover was about as far away from a flying assignment as the Air

Force could get him. It just didn't make sense: spend a million dollars to train a guy to fly, then send him to this desert hole in a nonflying job.

Sure, he knew the rationale: only a pilot could effectively run a base command post.

And only monkeys could effectively eat bananas, too.

Wendover AFB required a pilot in the command post as much as the Sahara needed sand. There just wasn't any need for it. If Wendover had a flying unit, it might make sense. The closest thing to flying Wendover had was the helicopter squadron—and they flew only to support Alpha Base security.

Helicopters. The word tasted bitter in McGriffin's mouth. Helicopter pilots went through a glorified six-month training course at Fort Rucker—an *Army* base—and called themselves pilots. They even wore the same wings as real pilots. McGriffin shook his head. Flying helicopters was as different from piloting a jet as driving a car.

The only consolation about this assignment was that he was away from Linda. When she had left him, it was hard enough having her move in with that aerospace guy—a nonflyer to boot! And for him to run across her in Tacoma—every time he went into town he dreaded the possibility that he'd see her; he had even changed churches, fearful that he might catch a glimpse of her . . . her red hair, laughing . . . there were too many memories.

At least here he'd have a chance to get over her. And from the looks of the sparse female population, he wasn't in any danger of latching on to someone while he was on the rebound.

Setting his jaw, he rang the buzzer on the door to the command post.

A disembodied voice came over a speaker. "Good

morning, sir. Could you hold your ID up to the mirror?"

McGriffin pulled out his wallet. He held the green ID up to the one-way mirror.

"Thank you, sir. Please step away from the door."

McGriffin took an awkward step back as a security policeman held the door open for him. "This way, Major." They walked down a narrow hallway to another barred door.

"Sir, Chief Zolley will escort you into the command post area."

Two airmen, resplendent in their Class A's, white gloves, and ascots, stood on either side of the causeway. McGriffin nodded as he passed. The guards stood mute. A single enlisted man greeted him. The man appeared to be a few years older than he—close to forty—but even so, to have someone so young attain the highest enlisted rank impressed McGriffin. The man firmly shook hands with him.

"Major McGriffin, welcome to Wendover. I'm Chief Master Sergeant Zolley, NCO in charge of the command post. Colonel DeVries is waiting in the back. He'll call for you momentarily. Can I get you a cup of coffee?"

McGriffin shook his head. "No thank you, Chief. Caffeine makes me jumpy."

The senior enlisted man smiled. "How about a tour of the CP, then? It may be a few minutes until the colonel is ready."

"Great. Sounds good—especially if I'm going to be working here. Lead the way."

"This way, sir. But I'll need to have you stop off at the verification center."

Chief Zolley led McGriffin to the back of the command post. A black rectangular object resembling a microfiche reader sat on a desk. Zolley explained,

"We need to get a picture of your retina for positive identification. It's a new system we went to: no one can duplicate the pattern your blood vessels make in your eye. It's kind of like a fingerprint, except much more accurate."

Zolley held out a chair for him. "This will only take a second. If you'll look into the goggles . . ."

Moving his head to the plate, McGriffin squinted into the blackness. As his eyes adjusted, he made out a narrow lens and what appeared to be a flashbulb—

"What!" The bulb went off, startling him. McGriffin pulled back from the device, rubbing his eyes.

"Sorry, sir. If I'd told you what to expect, you might have blinked." Chief Zolley punched buttons on the device and helped McGriffin out of his seat.

McGriffin squinted. Red, yellow, and green splotches filled the room.

As Zolley led McGriffin to the front of the command post, an airman removed the film from the verification unit. Zolley noted McGriffin's wings. "I hear that you used to fly out of McChord, sir."

McGriffin rubbed his eye and blinked. Things began to swim back into view. "Best tour of my life. I flew 141's darn near everywhere they could go."

"I was a crew chief there for three years. Tacqma was quite a place." He led Major McGriffin into the command post area. They squeezed in between an array of computer terminals and stopped before a huge screen depicting an aerial map of Wendover AFB. To the right a computerized board listed the various squadrons and tenant units on the Air Force base: 2021st Maintenance Group, 37th Airbase Wing, 1977th Aerospace Rescue and Recovery Squadron, and the Sixth Security Police Group.

Unit emblems decorated the wall behind him, barely visible in the low light. A row of five clocks lined the wall. To his right a status board listed twenty-five critical areas on the base. McGriffin noted that twenty of the areas were located inside of the Alpha Base complex.

From the aerial map, McGriffin picked out the town of Wendover, Nevada, lying northwest of the base; Dugway Proving Grounds was to the east, and, barely visible on the map, the Hill Air Force gunnery range. The crater containing Alpha Base showed up as a small spot on Wendover Air Force Base.

Chief Zolley stopped before a desk in front of the main board. Enlisted personnel worked quietly in the background, answering phones and updating information into their computer terminals. A green light burned softly over the status board. Chief Zolley noticed McGriffin lingering over the aerial map. "This part of the country is mostly a dried-out lake bed."

"I noticed. It looks like the Gulf of Mexico with that white sand."

Chief Zolley grinned. "After a year here you'd wish you were there. If it wasn't for Salt Lake City being two hours away by interstate, we wouldn't have any visitors at all. Most of them drive from Salt Lake City to gamble in Nevada, so we get a bit of the spillover; that, and the Enola Gay Museum here on base . . . you know, the plane in World War Two that dropped the first atomic bomb? They actually trained here, so we get a fair amount of tourists."

A voice called out over the command post. "Major McGriffin, the base commander requests your presence."

McGriffin straightened and flashed Chief Zolley a quick smile. "I'm looking forward to working with you, Chief."

"So am I, sir."

McGriffin turned for the exit. An airman stood by the door. "This way, Major." The airman held out a white-gloved hand, directing McGriffin out of the command post area.

Ducking into a hallway, McGriffin strode past several doorways: COMMUNICATIONS, NEST & BROKEN ARROW LIAISON, and BASE COMMANDER were posted on the walls. The enlisted guide stopped before the last door. He rapped sharply. When a voice answered, the guide nodded McGriffin in. "Major McGriffin, sir."

Colonel DeVries rocked back in his chair and surveyed McGriffin before answering. McGriffin noticed that the base commander was nonrated, a nonpilot. DeVries allowed a few unspoken moments to pass before he stood, leaving the chair bouncing in his wake. "Morning, Major. Welcome to Wendover." He extended a hand. "Charley DeVries."

"Thanks, sir. Bill McGriffin."

"Have a seat."

McGriffin pulled up a chair as DeVries walked behind his desk. "So you're from McChord. A 141 driver?"

"Yes, sir."

"We get quite a few 141's in here, carrying in nukes to store in Alpha Base. Ever been to Wendover, Bill?"

McGriffin turned in his chair. "No, sir. For the most part I just ferried trash across the pond."

DeVries smiled at McGriffin's nickname for the Pacific Ocean. "This will be a change of pace for you, then. We're a little different here from most bases you've been to. Wendover was used after World War Two as a test base—they used the salt flats and seclusion to practice taking off on short runways. In fact, we've got a war memorial here that's open to the public. As a result, there's a lot of tourists around, kind of unusual for our mission nowadays. The base was deactivated after the war, then reopened ten years ago when Alpha Base was built." He swiveled his chair around and pointed to a map of Wendover AFB hanging on the wall.

"Alpha Base was built to house America's stockpile of nuclear weapons. It's roughly seventy-five square miles of storage space, five miles due west of Wendover's main complex. Alpha Base is actually a base within a base, complete with its own security and barracks, taking up only a small fraction of Wendover's twenty thousand total square miles.

"The crater provides a way to keep watch on all the storage bunkers at once. All they had to do was to fence off the crater—the storage bunkers are burrowed into the crater's side. After the INF and strategic limitation agreements, Alpha Base was agreeable to the Soviets as the place to house our weapons."

McGriffin frowned. "Agreeable to the Soviets?"

"Their satellites fly overhead nearly once an hour, and with our good weather, they don't have to worry about clouds covering the storage sites—you know, so they can monitor activity here. It blows the dispersion policy for operational readiness all to hell, but we have the same arrangement with the Soviets at their storage site." McGriffin nodded as Colonel DeVries continued. "Over thirty thousand warheads are contained within Alpha Base's perimeter."

McGriffin whistled. "You must have some security detail guarding it."

"We do. It's a crackerjack outfit. In reality, there's so many checks to the high-tech security system, it's mostly a baby-sitting job."

DeVries turned back to his desk and scanned a sheet of paper. "You'll be rotating the command post duty with two other officers. Since you're the new kid on the block, I've assigned you to the night shift—1800 to 0200." He shoved the paper across the desk to McGriffin. "I hate to throw you right into the job, but we're low on help around here. Any problem starting your duty tonight?"

McGriffin's eyes widened. "No, sir. I guess not."

"Good." DeVries stood and extended his hand. "Glad to have you."

"Thanks, Colonel."

As McGriffin turned to leave, DeVries called after him. "Bill?"

"Sir?"

DeVries nodded his head toward McGriffin. "Nice hairs—but they won't hack it at my base. You aren't flying trash haulers anymore."

"I was just going to get a haircut this afternoon, sir."

"That's what I like to hear." DeVries turned to a pile of paper on his desk.

Red-faced, McGriffin turned on his heel, executing the first perfect about-face he'd done since he was a dooley.

2

Wednesday, 1 June, 0830 local

Wendover AFB

White noise washed over the area. Vikki Osborrn scrutinized the craft as it taxied off the end of the runway to the east of them. Although the plane was half a mile away, the sound from the jet's engines made it impossible to speak. A truck with an oversized sign exclaiming FOLLOW ME led the shrieking jet across an access road and past ten armored vehicles. Dozens of men clutching M-16's stood vigil along the plane's route.

Engines running, the camouflaged aircraft slowly pivoted on the concrete apron. Sand, kicked up from the exhaust, swirled overhead in crazy patterns. A uniformed airman decked out in green-brown battle-dress uniform and wearing earphones held two bright orange flashlights. He kept his left arm parallel to the ground and urged the plane to keep turning with his right. Through the jet's multifaceted window, the pilot kept his eyes glued on the airman until the airman crossed both arms over his head. The engines cut back and started winding down.

When the plane's engines grew quiet, Dr. Anthony Harding spoke.

"Have you found it?"

Vikki flipped through *Jane's All the World's Aircraft,* a large book filled with pictures of aircraft from every nation. "Not yet. I've found something like it—a C-5—but it looks too wide."

Harding glanced over at the book she held, then squinted back at the jet. "Keep looking—it's got to be in there."

Vikki pushed her hair back. Bleached from the sun, long blond hair adorned her tan face. She'd cause a man's head to turn, but only once. The appearance of glamor was striking, but up close the seriousness in her eyes overwhelmed the rest of her face. Upon inspection, the initial low twenties guess for her age melted to a figure closer to thirty-five.

Premature wrinkles tattooed the area around her eyes, and her skin had started to show the effect of too much sun—in a few years her skin would take on the leathery look that cursed those who worked in the field. Her tank top fit nicely, revealing small, rounded breasts. She crossed her legs and nervously bounced her sandals against the van's interior.

Harding turned back to the plane. Along with the rest of the tourists gawking at the convoy, Harding and Vikki were inconspicuous in the long line of cars that were stopped by the runway. He studied the plane. "There are ten armored vehicles, two flatbeds, and about seventy-five men—all with automatic weapons. Not counting the fuel trucks, I'd guess the armored vehicles each have bazookas and various

15

other nasty weapons on them." He lifted his glasses and rubbed his eyes.

Vikki stopped flipping through the pages. She squinted at one of the photographs, comparing it to the plane off to their right. "I've found it."

Harding moved the binoculars back to his eyes. "Well?"

"C-141B Starlifter, cargo aircraft of the U.S. Air Force," she recited. "Twenty-nine-hundred mile range, with a max payload of 91,000 pounds, and a top airspeed of 570 miles per hour." She looked up. "So what does that tell us?"

"Not much," answered Harding, "except if we can believe the intelligence NUFA gave us, the next time a C-141 lands at Wendover, chances are it will either be loading or unloading nuclear weapons. And if we're going to steal one of them, this is the time to do it."

"Are you crazy? Look at the mouseketeers out there. They've got this place locked up tighter than Alcatraz. I don't want to die doing something stupid."

Harding was silent for a moment. Vikki narrowed her eyes at him. She studied his dark, squat features. His once solid body had given way to a slight paunch. The wire-framed glasses added to the studious look. Gray peppered his hair, and a large bald spot adorned his head. He was on the wrong side of forty, and looked more like Vikki's father than her lover.

She scanned the concrete apron where activity began to pick up. Armored trucks encircled the C-141, reminding her of covered wagons closing in to keep attacking Indians away. A hundred and fifty years and they're still using the same tactics, she thought. Men scurried around the plane and took their positions on the ground, prone, with their weapons pointed outward. In the distance four helicopters hovered, not moving from their posts. Sun reflected off a deserted hangar behind the apron.

Harding spoke to himself. "They certainly are covering all the bases."

"What?"

Harding pointed to the helicopters Vikki had just noticed. "They're guarding the C-141 from the air as well as the ground. They don't want to chance anything going wrong."

Military police stood at a roadblock, blocking traffic to allow operations to continue. A police car sat off to the side of the road.

The C-141 sat on a pad, north of Vikki and Harding; the runway was east of them, and Alpha Base to the west. Vikki could barely make out the town of Wendover fifteen miles north of the C-141.

She leaned her head out the window. No breeze blew in the dry desert air. Heat rippled up from the road.

The flatbeds positioned themselves behind the C-141's gaping rear door. White, oversized barrels were carefully taken from the aircraft and gingerly strapped onto the flatbed, anchored by a series of straps and cables, keeping them upright and secure against tilting. Each barrel took less than a minute to position. After ten minutes the first flatbed pulled away to allow the second one access.

Once the drums were securely fastened to the second flatbed, two armored personnel carriers drove away from the plane, followed by the two flatbeds. A Ford Bronco, resplendent with machine guns and an official-looking flag waving from the front, sped in front of the convoy.

The convoy inched west down the main road. Several armed men guarded the route. Scanning the area, they kept close watch for anything that might approach the convoy.

Once the convoy had passed, security policemen started waving the traffic on. Vikki started the van. "What now?"

Harding pointed to the road. "Just follow the convoy."

Vikki put the Chevy van into gear and started slowly off, heading west.

"You had better begin thinking fast," she said, nodding ahead of her. "They're sending one of the guards to stop us."

A security policeman stepped from the side of the road and stopped the cars following the convoy. He walked straight toward them.

The guard sauntered up to the van. He shouldered his rifle and grinned at Vikki, all but ignoring Harding. "Afternoon, ma'am."

Harding leaned past Vikki. "Good afternoon, sir. What seems to be the problem?"

The security policeman looked surprised. "You don't have to call me sir. I'm not an officer or anything." He didn't look at Harding when he spoke, but instead smiled at Vikki.

Vikki furrowed her eyebrows. "What's the holdup? Are we doing anything wrong?"

"You'll have to wait here until the convoy gets back on the road." The security policeman pointed down a dry arroyo. "The bridge can't take the convoy's weight, so they have to drive down into the arroyo. Once they're back on the main road, you can proceed."

"Thanks," Vikki said, smiling.

The man tried to make conversation. "Heading for the picnic area?"

Harding answered before Vikki could open her mouth. "Yes, sir." He nodded to Vikki. "My sister and I are visiting the base and wanted to get some pictures of the crater before we left."

The security policeman hitched the rifle a little higher on his shoulder when Harding referred to Vikki as his sister. "Well, Alpha Base is certainly the spot to take pictures. It's the free world's largest storage facility. The picnic grounds are right outside the main gate. Are you planning to stay long?"

"That depends," said Harding.

The man looked behind him as the convoy reached the other side of the arroyo and started up on the paved road. "I have to get back, we're moving out. If there's anything I can do for you, let me know . . ." he trailed off, looking to Vikki hopefully.

Vikki shook her head and smiled. "Thanks, but we can manage."

As he headed off, Harding slumped back in his seat, smiling. "Alpha Base: the free world's largest storage facility! They're almost begging us to ask them for information. They don't go to this type of trouble for conventional explosives."

He tapped his fingers together. "Alpha Base. I've read about it in *Aviation Week and Space Technology,* but it's nice to get confirmation from a credible source."

Vikki snorted. "Some source—a nineteen-year-old militarist."

"He's just like any other nineteen-year-old in the world: lonely, and horny as hell. Which means we'll have to be careful, since he probably memorized your face. We don't want to bring any more attention to ourselves than we have to." Harding looked thoughtful. "That gives me an idea on how we can penetrate this base."

"I thought you wanted to create a diversion and get the nukes when they were unloading them."

Harding grinned and patted Vikki on the leg. Her thigh was firm, without an ounce of fat. "Don't worry. I've got an idea on how we can get into this base without raising any suspicions. If I'm right, they'll be thanking you for coming on base."

They followed a mile behind the convoy, slowly moving along the winding road. A line of cars followed them, no one anxious to risk passing the armed convoy along the way. Vikki made careful notes of the terrain as they drove. After the arroyo, clumps of piñon pine and cactus pocked the desert landscape. A golf course lay off to the right, its green fairways contrasting with the barren desert. A trail paralleled the main road, furrowed with the marks of off-road vehicles.

As they approached Alpha Base, her thoughts drifted to East Avenue, birthplace of the nukes . . .

The crowd surged along the avenue, pushing, laughing. They marched arm in arm, past vineyards that sweltered in the mid-August sun, holding up traffic and keeping the scientists from going to work. Sixty thousand people joined the carnivallike protest outside of Lawrence Livermore National Laboratory, the first demonstration this size in years.

Rows of wire fences funneled the protestors down the street, toward the nuclear weapons laboratory's main gate. A rock band on a flatbed, one hundred yards behind the crowd, belted out "Face the Fire," Dan Fogelberg's quintessential protest song.

Vikki Osborrn threw her long blond hair back and closed her eyes, laughing, and allowed the crowd to carry her along. Northern California, summertime, the drugs, the movement: it seemed so, so . . . *perfect,* so *right* to participate in the most wonderful, the most down-to-earth, the most *necessary* and critical activity that she could ever have imagined. She felt one with the crowd, and just *knew* that they would succeed, bring the nation's death factories to their knees.

A hand squeezed her shoulder, a separate sensation from the jostling that permeated the crowd. Opening her eyes, Vikki saw Dr. Anthony Harding; she smiled as a torrid memory of last night raced through her mind. The reminiscence was fogged in a marijuana haze, but the excitement and enthusiasm still shined through.

She turned her shoulder and slipped an arm around Harding. Her hand ran under his backpack and down his side, feeling hard, firm muscles. It had been his mind, his intellectual prowess, that had first drawn her to him; but that seemed nothing now compared with his physique, strong and protective. She had never been happier.

He had been elusive earlier this morning, teasing her about something special that was to happen. She was swept up in the protest now, eager just to experience whatever it was that he had promised.

Harding's arm enveloped her. He drew her close and spoke into her ear, over the crowd noise. "What do you think?"

"Perfect."

Harding took her by the shoulders; his eyes seemed to shine. His voice sounded a little loud, cocky, even over the crowd. "It's about time we started getting serious again, trying to stop the nuke factories. Even after the freeze movement petered out, glasnost and the peace dividend should have closed this place years ago." He shook his head. "What a waste. All these bright minds in one place, the opportunity to work on something really worthwhile, and what do they do? Spend their lives chasing after new ways to refine their weapons. And all they have to show for it is the Lawrence Award."

East Avenue continued to fill with people, a dancing mob surging without constraint. The sweet smell of hashish drifted across the crowd, mixing in with wine and beer. A chant started to ripple across the crowd.

"N-U-F-A . . . Nuke Free America today! N-U-F-A . . . Nuke Free America today!"

Vikki brought her hands up and started clapping. She screamed at the top of her lungs, joining in.

The crowd stopped in front of the main gate, squeezing up against the fences. Harding removed his backpack and held it tightly against his chest. Uniformed Department of Energy guards stood quietly just inside the gate and watched the throng of people. Remote-control TV cameras set on top of buildings panned across the crowd.

Vikki jumped up and down, her blond hair flying from side to side. Young, dedicated, and filled with a lust for life. She couldn't ask for anything more. And even the sight of Dr. Anthony Harding, coolly watching the guards on the other side of the fence, couldn't shake her from the feeling.

She turned to Harding and brushed back her hair. "Anthony—"

"Hold this." Harding shoved the backpack at her. He held what appeared to be three black balls. The crowd around them surged toward the main gate.

Vikki frowned. Since she was high, it took some effort to understand what Harding was doing; she held the backpack to her breasts. "Anthony, what are you doing?"

Harding grinned, the sun shining off his premature bald spot. "Get ready to run like hell." He knelt down and rapidly pulled pins from each of the three balls.

Vikki pushed back against the crowd. "Anthony?"

Harding stood, scanned the area, then drew back and threw one of the balls as hard as he could. He let go of the remaining two just as quickly; the balls flew high into the air, tumbling in an arc. "Come on!" He grabbed her elbow and started pushing through the crowd.

"Ooof!" Vikki was hit in the side of her face by an elbow; she kicked out and held on to Harding's hand. The crowd continued to jump up and down, unmindful of their flight.

Brrooooooom! Brrooooooom, brroooooooom. Screams —the three explosions set the crowd scurrying backward. People fell, were trampled as the horde panicked.

Sirens, bells, the smell of smoke. Vikki and Harding were halfway through the crowd, keeping up their momentum. Most of the people tried moving in random directions, unmindful of any obstacles in their path. The wire fences channeled back along East Avenue, away from the golden brown hills surrounding the valley.

Harding continued to drag her along. It seemed like a nightmare, the screaming and cries for help pounding into her ears.

Harding stopped when they reached the vineyards, just outside of the Livermore complex. They turned and watched the people stream past. Smoke billowed up from a building just inside the nuclear weapons laboratory. Alarm bells and sirens ran up the scale as a fire truck inside the fence attempted to quell the blaze.

As they watched, Vikki felt a sudden sense of accomplishment.

Something swelled inside her. She clasped hands with Harding and watched. Guards openly brandished weapons now, shoving people away from the laboratory, beating them over the head. Garbled orders emanated from bullhorns.

They *had* brought the death factory to its knees. The feeling overwhelmed her, the sense of power . . . of, of *righteousness*. To think that Dr. Anthony Harding had fought, had *won!*

And she knew that her life was forever changed.

She finally had a purpose. . . .

Harding pointed to Alpha Base. "They're stopping traffic again while they open the gate."

The guards dispersed from the APC's and lined the main gate to Alpha Base. The Bronco led the two flatbed trucks onto the complex, moving past four barbed-wire fences. Men trotted into the area and formed up in a block. Once inside, the gates swung shut and traffic began to move. The flatbeds seemed to disappear into the ground.

Harding squinted at a sign near the entrance. "Turn left. The picnic area is down that way." Approaching Alpha Base, they climbed to the lip of the crater.

Vikki crept passed the main gate complex while Harding took copious notes. "It looks like one of the fences is electrified. And from the signs they've got posted, they probably have the place wired with sensors."

Vikki pulled into a grassy area fifty yards from the fences; a sign read, ALPHA BASE PICNIC AREA P-1. Other cars followed them. A group of youngsters spilled from the automobiles. The kids wore colored stockings, matching shirts and shorts. A few of the children carried soccer balls. A beleaguered adult yelled shrilly and tried to get the kids to gather around him.

Vikki slumped back in her seat. "Well, what do you think?"

Harding pointed to the flatbed trucks inside the fence. From their vantage point, Alpha Base spread below them, the crater opening up in a giant yawn. The flatbeds stopped before one of the bunkers. A steel door swung slowly open, allowing access, and affording them a quick glimpse inside.

Harding whistled. "Those bunkers look impossible to break into."

Vikki was silent for a moment as they watched the white canisters being moved from the flatbeds to the bunker. "Are you going back to your original plan of hijacking the convoy?"

"Not with all that security. They've got those nukes covered tight."

"But you just said it's impossible to break into the bunkers."

Harding pointed inside the fence. "It is. But look at those security policemen."

Vikki leaned over the steering wheel. "They're pretty relaxed."

"That's right. Inside the fence, they're in their own territory. They're safe, and they know it. They don't need to be as alert. And this picnic ground—if they let kids from military families up here, you know they think they're safe." He reached over and unfastened her seat belt. "Step outside."

"Huh?"

"Go ahead, get out of the van."

Vikki frowned, but stepped from the Chevy van and kept the door open. She held a hand up over her eyes and slowly scanned Alpha Base. She nodded to a group of airmen horsing around just inside the fences. Vikki called to Harding: "I wouldn't think they would be so casual."

"That's what's going to make our chances better. The way to rip off the nuclear weapons is to do it right

25

under their noses. We break into Alpha Base when they least expect it and blow one of the bunkers."

Vikki looked disgusted. "I'm sure you're going to waltz up to the gate and ask, 'Pretty please, can I have one of your nukes?' Get real, Anthony. Are you going to call this thing off or not?"

Inside the fence one of the security policemen elbowed a buddy and waved at the van.

Harding urged Vikki, "Go ahead and wave back to him. I've got a plan how this whole thing will fall together. In fact, you're the key to how we get onto Alpha Base."

"I'm not sure if I like what you're thinking," Vikki said. "Look at those Neanderthals—slobbering over each other trying to get my attention."

"Keep waving. After we leave, I'll fill you in with all the details."

Vikki forced an insincere smile for the men and waved once more before climbing back in the van. "Let's get the hell out of here. If I'm sacrificing my body, I want to know how you plan to do it." She thought to herself that Harding was getting more difficult to live with; it wasn't like the days when they were younger.

It had better be one hell of a plan.

3

Wendover AFB Command Post

Chief Zolley walked McGriffin to the exit. When they reached the corridor, Chief Zolley shooed the security policeman out, saying, "I'll see Major McGriffin to the door."

"Very well, Chief." The man slung his rifle over his shoulder and headed into the command post area. He eyed Zolley. "Mind if I take a smoke break?"

Zolley waved him on. "Go ahead. This will take a few minutes—I've got to brief the major on some additional procedures."

Once the door slammed and they were alone, Chief Zolley turned to McGriffin. "Anything else I can help you with, sir?"

"I don't think so. It looks pretty quiet around here."

"It is. Alpha Base is mostly automated, as far as

27

security goes. It's got so many gee-whiz bells and whistles it will make your head spin. The guards rely on electronics to keep them apprised of what's going on. As a result, we don't do anything here except transfer their messages to Washington."

McGriffin nodded. "Chief, I'm reporting for duty at 1800 tonight. I assume you'll be here to help me learn the ropes?"

"Great, sir. I think you'll enjoy it. It's not the real Air Force, but then again, I don't think you can find the real Air Force anywhere. I've assigned myself to your shift for the next month. I wanted to make sure I could help out if you needed me."

"You already have." McGriffin firmly shook Zolley's hand. "I'm looking forward to working with you and your men."

Chief Zolley cracked a smile. "The pleasure's all yours, Major."

McGriffin grasped the door leading to the outside and pressed on. He strode into the brilliant Utah sunshine.

Helicopters swung out from the base, practicing landings in the desert. Their chopping came as a low beat in the distance. From the front of the command post it seemed as if Wendover AFB were just another lazy western town. The absence of traffic and bustling people gave the base a feeling of mañana. Even Alpha Base's presence a few miles away could not shake the sanguine atmosphere bubbling in the sunshine.

This might not be so bad, thought McGriffin. I might grow to enjoy this place. Even if I'm not flying.

1215 local

Wendover, Nevada

Dr. Anthony Harding wiped up his enchilada combination plate with a sopapilla. Yellow egg yolk spotted the plate, mixed in with shredded lettuce, refried beans, sour cream, green chile, and salsa. He drained his beer and wiped his mouth before speaking. "Where did you find the apartment?"

Vikki studied him before answering. She'd have to get on him about his table manners—he looked like a slob. And slobs bring attention to themselves. "Second and Main. It's about thirty minutes from the base. I could have gotten closer, but most of the apartments were real sleaze bags. If I'm going to impress these GI Joes, I thought I should try to find something a little more upscale."

"Don't get anything too fancy. Remember, you're supposed to be a secretary." Harding belched. "I picked up some maps from the park service. There's a wooded area in the mountains about two hours from here—around Matterhorn Peak in Humboldt National Forest. I'll check it out first thing tomorrow. It just might do for the staging area."

He patted his jacket pocket and pulled out a small notebook. He flipped through the pages and accidentally knocked a fork off the table. "What places are you going to hit tonight?"

"Anthony, pay attention to what you're doing. People are starting to stare."

"Let them."

Vikki swirled her margarita and looked away. The small Mexican restaurant proudly exclaimed, "Hon-

29

We Ain't." Lunchtime, and the small restaurant was jam-packed with patrons.

Vikki ran her fingers over the tabletop, tracing out small swirls in the water left from her drink. "There's a place called Shotgun Annie's. From the looks of it, it should be a military hangout: rock band, no cover for women, and two-for-one beers until nine. I'll straighten the apartment tonight and hit it tomorrow."

Harding held his hand up for another beer. "That reminds me." They grew quiet as a couple walked past. When the waitress arrived with the beer, he drained half of it. "The security policemen: they're the key to the whole operation." He took a healthy sip and eyed Vikki over the salted rim. "It's crucial you gain their confidence. Get one of the guards to trust you, and we'll find a way into Alpha Base."

Vikki drew in a deep breath and nodded. "I understand." She looked up and wiped a strand of hair from her eyes. "Don't worry about me—I can handle it. Just don't you screw up."

Harding grinned and held the glass up to his mouth. In the background the jukebox wailed a Mexican song. The waitress slid over and shoved the tab onto the table. The paper whirled between Vikki and Harding. Harding said, "Do whatever you have to do, Vikki."

She stared through him, unblinking.

Do what ever you have to do, Vikki. The words came back to her.

They were younger then, and more idealistic. Anthony didn't have his paunch, and as a post-doc at Berkeley, he had swept her off her feet the first time they met. Until she learned of his background.

Vikki had lived in Berkeley since her undergraduate days, never wanting to relinquish the university crowd. It was safe, secure. One degree had led to another—Art, English, Food Sciences—and as the degrees piled up, so did the years.

It was as if she had never really found herself. She had always been looking for a cause, from her high school days in Colorado digging into the environmental issues, to the People's Republic of Berkeley, leading the activist movement to bring socialism to the city.

But it wasn't until the post-nuclear freeze movement, NUFA—Nuclear Free America—had caught her attention that she finally really felt part of something. She immersed herself in the activities, attended all the meetings, sat through all the inciting speakers, but still had never committed herself to anything more than just being a member.

Until she met Anthony Harding.

She fell for him, then discovered his Ph.D. from Cal Tech was in nuclear physics, and that abhorred her. She looked at him as an evil wizard, summoning up demons and unseen gargoyles. *Nuclear* was as inciting then as *pig, the man,* or *the heat* was in the sixties. If it was nuclear, it was bad. It must be destroyed.

Myopic technocrats tried to push *nuclear* down the people's throats. They surged past reason, circumvented rational thinking, all in the name of the almighty dollar.

It didn't take Vikki long to introduce Harding to NUFA.

The arguments advanced by Nuclear Free America were compelling, but Harding did not quickly become a sympathetic listener. He argued he didn't *build* bombs, he just did research with quarks, gluons, and other elementary particles. Researching basic physics was not the same as designing bombs, bombs that killed without prejudice, vaporizing babies as well as soldiers.

But it set Harding thinking.

The Livermore debacle proved that he was sincere.

The annual protests at the nuclear weapons laboratory made for an ideal setting. Situated forty miles from Berkeley, the nuclear bomb factory permeated death. The computer center—home of the monstrous behemoths with strutting, smirking names like Cray and ETA—whipped up a frenzy among the NUFA idealists. Weapons physicists with nicknames like the "Montana Madman," "Raunchy Rhoades," "T-T," and "Jimmy L." were the purveyors of death: without their computers to design the nukes, there would be no nuclear weapons.

Harding became obsessed with the death factory; NUFA incited him to the breaking point.

So three grenades, whipped high over the fence on East Avenue, put a temporary stop to the nuclear madness, completely destroying the computer center. And drove Vikki and Harding into the L.A. underground.

There wasn't a challenge to bring them to the surface—nothing important to make them appear. Until now.

Until Alpha Base.

Harding needed it. Vikki needed it more. And she was willing to put up with anything to see it through.

She'd slept with Harding that first month to help bring him around to NUFA's ways. Offering her body to him didn't make him change his mind, change his philosophy about nuclear weapons; but it provided the motivation for him to listen.

She did it once—she could do it again.

Vikki nodded absently and murmured to Harding, "Don't worry—I'll do what I have to do."

4

Major McGriffin looked over his empire. It wasn't much, but it was impressive as all get-out.

The darkened command post resembled a futuristic stage set: red lights reflected off the brows of the men and women seriously going about their jobs. McGriffin leaned back in his chair and reached for his cup of decaffeinated coffee.

One hour into the first day on the job, and the boredom was already driving him bananas. Adding to it, this Wendover assignment still irked him. As chief of the prestigious Standardization and Evaluation team at McChord Air Force Base outside of Tacoma, McGriffin was one of the "best of the best," charged with scrutinizing the flying abilities of the other pilots. He made sure that a USAF pilot was for real: precise, exacting, and meticulous.

But Military Personnel Command decried that pilots couldn't compete, and wouldn't get promoted, unless they did something other than flying. His orders soon followed: an assignment to Wendover on a "rated supplement" tour—an assignment designed to supplement his rated, or flying, status.

Now he could compete with the other officers when it came time for promotions. And Wendover would have a rated officer to operate its command post.

Never mind that the nation would not have the use of an experienced pilot flying the Air Force's workhorse cargo plane; and never mind that the experience level of combat-trained pilots was at an all-time low. Major William McGriffin was doing something *much* more important: filling a slot that anyone could do.

McGriffin darkly suspected that the Air Force Military Personnel Command was a clandestine arm of the Soviet KGB. After all, what better way to drive experienced pilots out of the Air Force, and thus degrade the war-fighting ability, than to assign pilots to nonflying jobs?

The one consolation was that the command post practically ran itself, and whenever something happened, Chief Zolley was right there at his elbow, offering a suggestion about what to do.

McGriffin rocked forward in his chair. "Chief Zolley?"

"Yes, sir?" The sergeant appeared behind him.

"What's the catch?"

"Sir?"

McGriffin drained his cup of decaf and banged it on the table. "It took me all of ten minutes for your in-processing briefing, and there isn't a thing going on tonight. Is the command post usually this quiet, or does some earth-shaking excitement come around once every hundred years?" He motioned for Zolley to sit.

Zolley smiled gently, sipping on his coffee. "Actually, sir, it's kind of unusual for an officer to take command of a CP this early in his tour. The Operating Instructions calls for an extended period of on-the-job training—following the officer of the day around until all the procedures are down pat. Kind of an OJT program for field graders." He lifted his coffee and swirled it around before taking a sip.

McGriffin opened his mouth when the siren went off.

"ThreatCon Delta, I say again, ThreatCon Delta: there is a break-in at Alpha Base!"

McGriffin fell backward in the scramble. The board outlining Alpha Base lit up in bright yellow. A quarter of the way around the map a red spot blinked angrily.

Chief Zolley helped McGriffin to his feet and took his elbow, easing him to the front of the control desk. An enlisted man jammed a telephone to Zolley's ear. He said, "Chief Zolley, I have contact with the NEST and Broken Arrow teams, DNA, and the Security Council. They are waiting on conference call." The airman hesitated and glanced over to McGriffin.

Zolley took the phone and spoke quickly to McGriffin. He covered the mouthpiece with a hand. "We need to keep Washington apprised of everything that's going on, sir. I can handle it if you prefer . . ."

McGriffin nodded, his eyes wide. "Go ahead, I'm still a bystander."

"Thank you, Major. But I may need you if Washington requires an on-site command decision."

"Take it, Chief. I'll trust your judgment."

"Thanks, sir." Zolley flipped on the intercom button and walked toward the map of Alpha Base, stopping just on the far side of the desk. The phone line trailed behind him, its cord making a spaghettilike pattern. He squinted at the computer display as information raced across the screen. He spoke into the phone.

"Washington, this is Wendover CP. We've gone to ThreatCon Delta with an alarm at station Foxtrot Two One. Motion sensors Foxtrot Alpha Five and Foxtrot Alpha Thirty-Two have picked up the motion and registered a coincidence of zero point nine nine on penetration. Number of intruders is indeterminate, but not expected to exceed three. Mobile units have been dispatched. Recommend a visual before lowering ThreatCon level."

"Concur, Wendover. I roger that. Let's do a wait-and-see."

Chief Zolley put down the phone and kept his eyes glued to the screen. McGriffin inched around to where Chief Zolley stood, and watched in silence. Zolley pointed with the telephone to the computer readout.

"Washington is getting the same information flashed to them from the Alpha Base command post. By reading it back to them I give them an oral verification on their sensor status. If they need anything done, they'll ask our opinion first—and then do whatever the hell they want to do."

"What's going on?"

"Probably nothing. They get these breaks in the system all the time. Besides, if it were serious, we'd have been getting more sensor data by now. Probably just an animal."

McGriffin relaxed minutely. The atmosphere still seemed tense in the command post, but it didn't have the same edge as when the alarm first went off. Most of the room crowded around the monitor. Everyone was quiet, waiting for word from Alpha Base.

McGriffin leaned back on the desk and folded his arms. "You really think an animal could have set off all those alarms?"

"Most probably. All they need to do is get inside the first fence and they're spotted. Once the alarm goes off, it scares the hell out of them and they usually get out of there. Now, if it were something bigger, like a bear or a human, then there would be an even bigger commotion."

"A bear?" McGriffin eyed Zolley, not sure if the chief master sergeant was pulling his leg or not.

"All clear!" An obnoxious bell rang, breaking the tension. The room laughed, then everyone slowly went back to work. It reminded McGriffin of a fire alarm: people were glad it was over, but they still felt uneasy.

Zolley spoke rapidly on the phone. "Confirm another rabbit, and a hole has been spotted in the first fence, approximately three inches in diameter. The civil engineers have been dispatched and escorts provided for repair work. This is Wendover, end transmission." He handed the phone over.

"Well, what do you think, sir?"

"Impressive." McGriffin swept his eyes over the facility, then turned his attention back to the map of Alpha Base. Once again the lights glowed a soft green.

The map showed Alpha Base as a crater, five miles west of the Wendover main complex. Four white lines twisted around the perimeter, delineating the fences encircling the nuclear weapons storage facility. Points dotted the map, marking sensor locations. Foxtrot Alpha Five and Foxtrot Alpha Thirty-Two, the two sensors responsible for detecting the rabbit, were lost in the jumble of dots.

"How often do these alarms occur?"

Zolley shrugged. "Not more than once or twice a

month. Washington actually likes them. It keeps everyone on their toes and ensures the communications gear is working."

McGriffin shot a glance at the clocks mounted on the wall. Five digital timepieces displayed five different time zones. One read LOCAL, and showed Utah time: currently 1932.

The other clocks reminded him of flying: the names WASHINGTON, D.C. and ZULU—which denoted Greenwich Mean Time—were standard. He guessed that the clock marked OMAHA was there because of Strategic Air Command headquarters. The commander-in-chief of SAC would have a fit if the largest user of the nukes in Alpha Base wasn't apprised of what was going on.

But the one clock perpetually pointing to 1700 bothered him. Obviously broken, it either should be fixed or taken down, he thought. Below the clock was a cryptic name for a location he didn't recognize: MILLER. And something still nagged at him. The rabbit . . . no, it was that bear Chief Zolley had alluded to.

"Chief."

Zolley turned, papers in his grasp. "Sir?"

"About that bear. Were you pulling my leg, or did a bear really get in Alpha Base?"

Chief Zolley held up his hands. "Honest, sir. It was a baby bear cub, probably got lost from the mountains and wandered down here. It somehow managed to get past the first three fences."

"What happened?"

"It would have gotten to fence four—the electric one—if the security police hadn't scared it away, chased it several miles and blown it full of holes."

"A bear cub?"

Zolley nodded. "In fact, they were still finding bullets weeks after the incident in the housing area.

Some of the younger troops got overly excited and not only shot the poor cub up, but managed to unload quite a few rounds into base housing. We were lucky no one got killed. One colonel was nearly pumped full of lead when he went out to get his morning paper."

"Too bad. About the bear, I mean." As McGriffin stretched his arms, he had a sudden thought. "Chief . . ." McGriffin pointed to the clocks overseeing the chamber. "What's that fifth clock—the one marked 'Miller'?"

Zolley broke into a grin. "Somewhere in the world it's that time, all the time, sir."

"Miller time?" McGriffin looked puzzled, then groaned, remembering the beer commercial. "I get it." He waved an arm. "Back to work, you clowns!"

With his crew having a sense of humor, maybe things weren't going to be so bad around here after all.

5

Shotgun Annie's
Wendover, Nevada

The music was country rock—"post-outlaw," the kids called it. The twang was missing, as were the lyrics from the country music played in Nashville. Instead, a solid bass drove the melody, a lead riffed at just the right spot . . . which reminded Vikki of her Berkeley days, but more as something new, unconventional.

And the crowd was short-haired with elan, also different from her past. The group vibrated, energetic, wide open.

It was a far cry from the world she'd known.

She had grown up fast as an undergraduate, living in the Bay Area, and nearly killing herself with all the partying. Her first "Hairy Buffalo" party was a dim memory: gallons of wine, rum, vodka, beer, and whiskey poured in a bathtub and mixed together. She had indeed felt like a hairy buffalo after waking, and vowed to stay away from alcohol.

That lasted all of a week. After her first experiments with drugs, she was totally wasted for over a year.

If it wasn't for NUFA and finding a purpose in life, she would have probably killed herself. She'd done a lot of growing up then, rearranging her priorities. She discovered how committed she was after she met Harding. It took a while, but once she'd convinced him that NUFA's goals really were moral, he'd become more of a zealot than she. Since then she'd kept out of touch with the party scene. Shotgun Annie's was her first touch with a dance bar since Livermore.

Vikki ordered a Chablis and settled back, sipping and watching. A few groups clustered by themselves, leaving each other alone. The decor allowed a quiet tête-à-tête to exist without bringing attention to one another.

Smoke wafted across her table. Tobacco. It seemed strange not to smell the sweet hemp of marijuana, but again it was the crowd. They were much too cautious to air something like dope out in the open. The place was laconic, not defiant.

Another glass of wine confirmed her suspicions. Shotgun Annie's was definitely not a pickup bar. It was dark enough that someone should have made a pass in the last half hour. It was time for her to do something about it.

Vikki drained her glass and left a tip on the table. Flipping back her hair, she sauntered past the bar and into a back room set apart from the main area. Earlier, several husky men—all short hairs—had strode through the bar, avoiding eye contact with the rest of the patrons.

The back room grew quiet when she entered. A few

men looked at her; one elbowed his buddy, but most just ignored her. No one spoke—no greeting, pleasantries, or even a smile. It was as if she entered a private club and was being shunned.

She caught the eye of the man who had elbowed his friend. The man looked younger than the rest of his friends. His blond hair was cut in a longish crew cut. She held his stare momentarily, then purposely turned and walked out of the room.

She caught a few fragments of conversation from other places in the bar, but nothing came from behind her. The bartender walked over. He wiped his hands on a towel and placed his hands flat on the bar. "What can I get you?"

"White wine." Vikki kept her head turned away from the room she just left.

The bartender squatted and grasped a five-liter green bottle by the neck. The Wente Brothers Winery label on the front was waterlogged from condensation.

Vikki opened her purse to pay when a bill slid across the bar.

A voice came from behind her. "I've got it." The bartender snatched up the bill and turned to the cash register. "Keep it."

"Thanks." The bartender tucked the change under his apron.

Vikki picked up her glass and took a deliberate sip before turning. When she rotated around, the man's face came into view. Just as she thought—it was the young blond-haired man whose eye she had caught. She leaned back against the bar and took another sip before speaking.

"I don't usually let strangers, especially young ones, buy me a drink." She twirled the wine in her glass and said slowly, "And when they do, they're usually disappointed that I don't sleep with them."

The man's face widened into a grin. "You're honest. I guess you don't have to feel guilty about accepting my drink."

Vikki raised her wineglass in a mock salute. "No, I don't."

The man looked quickly around and pulled up a bar stool. He swiped a few crumbs away that had fallen from the counter. He settled onto the stool. He watched her for a moment before saying, "You look lonely."

"I'm not."

The man smiled slowly and stuck out a hand. "I'm George Britnell. I didn't catch your name."

"I didn't offer it."

Britnell raised an eyebrow. "Well, well. Not even for buying you a drink?"

Vikki smiled; an honest man. "Vikki Osborrn." She accepted his hand and gave him a firm handshake.

Britnell turned to the bartender. "Yo, 'keep. Lay a brew on me."

Vikki merely sipped her drink and studied him. Britnell couldn't be more than twenty. Tall, decent-looking, athletic build, probably about 180 pounds. Not like Harding—Harding's middle-age gut had started when he was about Britnell's age, while he was working in a physics lab. Harding didn't have a reason to keep fit. He had everything he wanted now, including her.

Too bad this young hunk didn't know any better. His morals were probably as deep as his navel. A lot was riding on this; she needed to play up to his ego.

Britnell drew on his beer. He watched Vikki for a moment, locking eyes with her. "So why did you come to the back room?"

Vikki shrugged. "Just checking out what's going on. What's so special about it?"

"You don't know?"

Vikki looked puzzled. "No, should I?"

Britnell pulled his stool closer to Vikki. "This is great. I mean, when a girl comes into the back, it's usually because they—well, are after someone who works in the Pit."

"The pit." Vikki put her glass down and traced her finger over the top of the bar. "Now you're talking nonsense."

Britnell laughed and drained his beer. He slid it across the bar top. "Another one, 'keep." He turned back to Vikki. "The *Pit,* my lady. It's the place where the toughest, the crème la de crème work—you know, the best of the best."

Vikki kept a straight face at his attempt at French. "And you work there."

Britnell just smiled. "That's right."

"I see." Vikki tried to look bored. She swiftly ran her eyes around Shotgun Annie's. She had to pull him along, ever so slowly. . . .

"Wait." Britnell looked worried. "Uh, how about you, are you from around here?"

Vikki smiled gently. "No, but I live here now. I work for one of the construction firms in town. We're bidding the Wendover construction upgrade."

"Where are you from?"

"California. The Bay Area."

"Hey, that's great. California. I always wanted to visit, but haven't found the time. I'm from Pennsylvania myself. Nevada's the farthest west I've ever been. This place is about as far from the hills and trees as you can get. We—I mean, I—work with a lot of really high-tech gear—in fact, the best. You know, maybe we have something in common."

Vikki picked up her glass. "Maybe we do." The bartender shoved another mug of icy draft in front of

Britnell. Vikki waited until he drained half of it before asking, "Tell me, George Britnell, why is a good-looking guy like you buying drinks for an older woman? Why don't you go after someone your own age?"

Britnell held up a finger to the bartender, already signaling for another one. He belched lightly. "There's something about you that knocked me out. You sure the hell didn't look that old when I first saw you." He flushed. "You know what I mean."

Vikki smiled tightly. "Tell me more about this high-tech business you're in. Maybe it is fascinating."

Britnell laughed. He grabbed for the beer pushed in front of him. "High-tech business. That's great."

Vikki sat with a smile painted on her face, waiting for Britnell to finish his third beer. She wanted him to talk, to tell her everything about himself. Britnell would never get close to her if she simply tried to pick him up; she had to cultivate a trust, stretch out the relationship so it wasn't just based on sex.

Which was important to her, too. The thought of prostituting her body, allowing her very essence to be used to further her goals, was something she didn't take lightly. The guilt from her past, growing up in the Bible-banging foothills of Colorado, was something she had overcome years ago. Or at least she had *tried* to overcome.

She looked upon using her body as a means for accomplishing ends; bringing Britnell into her confidence would take more than shaking her fanny at him. But if that's what it took to initiate the relationship, then she would put her thoughts and emotions aside. For what was more important to her—chastity, or showing the world how easy it was to steal nuclear weapons?

There was just no comparison.

She quietly slipped the bartender more than enough cash to cover the additional drinks and the tip. When Britnell drained the last drop, she stood and took him by the elbow.

"Hey—" he sputtered, not too coherently.

"Let's go to my place. I really do want to learn more about you." She led him out the door, and once he hit the night air, almost collapsed into her arms.

6

Wendover AFB's Hole in the Ground Grill

McGriffin sat munching an Army Air Force Exchange
Service grease burger: easy on the meat and heavy on
the grease. Actually, the sandwich had a lot going for
it. He'd first had the ubiquitous grease burger as an
undergraduate pilot training student at Laughlin
AFB, Texas. Every BX grill in the world boasted of it.

After stumbling in from a flight at zero dark early, it
was usually the only thing he could find at the AAFES
eatery. Heavy on the mayo, double pickles, and it
would fill you right up. That and a cherry Coke.

The hamburger hit the spot. It was like taking an old
friend around with him. All he needed to do now was
to fly.

An aero club was just around the corner—his
private pilot's license was still good, but he'd have to
wait until they were open. Likewise, there at least had

47

to be some sort of church fellowship around to get him introduced to the social scene. Things were looking up.

"Good morning, Major." Chief Zolley pulled out a chair at the next table.

McGriffin waved him over. "Have a seat."

"Thanks." Zolley plopped down across from McGriffin. He glanced at McGriffin's grease burger and shuddered.

Pushing back his plate, McGriffin leaned back against his chair. "If every night's like tonight, I'm going to have to find something to keep me from going crazy."

"It gets worse. At least tonight we had that killer rabbit attack."

"Great. I can see it now: three years of boredom punctuated with five minutes of terror."

Chief Zolley chewed on his sandwich before speaking. "Major, if I were you, I'd learn everything I could about our tenant units."

"Tenant units?"

"Yes, sir. All we do is keep house. You know, supply the security guards, hospital, civil engineers, golf course—that sort of thing. Since you command the CP, you'll come into contact with them one of these days. Besides, you might see something interesting."

McGriffin laughed in the middle of taking another bite. Choking, he brought up his napkin as he coughed. "I tried to stay as far away from those places as I could." He shook his head. "I'm lucky to have been able to fly as long as I did without doing anything else. This nonrated nonsense is all new to me."

"Really, sir, give it a chance. You ought to at least take a trip out to Alpha Base. Wendover wouldn't be here if it wasn't for them."

"We'll see." He dove back into his grease burger.

When Chief Zolley and McGriffin departed the AAFES snack bar, Zolley threw McGriffin a salute. "Good luck, sir."

"Are you sure they won't mind me snooping around?"

"Not at all. Once they know you're from the command post, they'll let you in with open arms. After all, they might need a favor someday."

"Thanks, Chief. I'll see you at 1800—I've got to get my body adjusted to this new schedule."

Saturday, 4 June, 2135 local

Wendover, Nevada

The apartment complex sat in a dark neighborhood two streets from Main Street. Vikki Osborrn entered the door with her arm wrapped around Britnell's waist. His youthful body felt firm. She grasped him tightly, uneasy about the place they entered.

She left her purse and sweater in the car. A bare bulb burned at the top of the stairs. As they negotiated the wooden stairway, the boards creaked, adding to the music leaking from the door at the top. A shrill cry of laughter pierced the air. Vikki made out the music as an old punk classic. She drew in a breath as Britnell opened the door.

The crowd barely noticed them.

Sleep with a comrade and you're one of the crowd, she thought. Britnell patted her fanny and squeezed his way to the drinks. Eight Air Force security policemen filled up the kitchen, popping beer, laughing. Most of the men had women standing next to them. The women listened, not talking, and smiled at the men's words.

49

Vikki sipped lightly at the glass of Chablis Britnell thrust to her. She brushed back her hair. "I want to look around. Be right back."

The women around her reeked of youth—eighteen-year-old girlfriends of immaculately sculptured airmen. The music blared. It was so loud she couldn't hear much more than garbled words over the monotone beats. One of the women—*girls!*—swayed slowly back and forth to the music, her eyes glazed over. Vikki gave a silent praise of thanks that the girls weren't popping gum.

One of the women approached her. Her smile was friendly enough, but yet as the girl looked her over, Vikki saw her eye linger on her face, no doubt taking in the telltale marks of age. The girl smiled warmly.

"I don't believe I've met you. I'm Daria."

Vikki extended a hand. "Vikki. Glad to meet you."

Daria sipped coyly on her wine. "I haven't seen you around. George has done well. Are you playing the Pit, or is he your first?"

Vikki looked puzzled. "Playing the pit?"

Daria glanced around at the faces of the other women who gathered around. She looked shocked. "Why surely you know that George works in the Pit?"

"Sure. What about it?"

Silence.

From the kitchen laughter split the solemn moment for an instant. Daria regained her composure and took another sip of wine. "You really don't know, do you?" Vikki just stared back at her. Daria put her drink down and grasped Vikki by the arm. "This is just so unusual, I'm really going to have to introduce you around."

She steered Vikki back past the kitchen and into a cramped living room. Music pulsated from two speakers at opposite ends of the room. Wire ran up the walls from the amplifier to each of the speakers. Daria raised her voice over the music.

"Hey, everybody—we've got a virgin!" Vikki rolled her eyes as Daria clicked off the amplifier. She stood unsteadily in the center of the room. "George's date is a virgin."

"Welcome to the club, sister. Put your name in the hat and grab a date."

"Sit down, Daria—you've had too much to drink."

Daria lifted her glass in a mock toast. "Well, George's date is free game, and I don't want anyone to spoil it for her."

A catcall accompanied Daria's reply. Daria stuck out her tongue at the group and paced back to Vikki. She looped her arm over Vikki's. Someone flicked back on the stereo.

Vikki shook her off. "What was that all about?" she demanded.

Daria laughed. "You, my dear, are an endangered species."

Vikki lowered her voice. *"You* are going to be endangered if you don't explain. What is going on?"

Daria sobered up at Vikki's tone. "The guys who work in the Pit—Alpha Base, to the uninitiated—are the top security policemen in the Air Force. They've been specially selected to work there. It's an honor assignment for them. Their Air Force career is in the bag, and they'll be getting choice jobs and assignments from here on out." She sipped unsteadily at her wine. "What I'm getting at is, if you can hook one of them, you're going places—you've got it made. And since you've never dated one of them before, you're a special commodity."

"What's so special about it?"

"For one thing, you're not a secondhand gal— jumping from one bed to the next. The guys tend to look up to you for that."

Vikki studied Daria. She wasn't drunk, but from the edge in her voice, Vikki could tell that she hit a nerve. Maybe it explained the tenseness in the room when she was around, Vikki thought. She decided to take a chance. She said coyly, "Not like you, I take it."

"That's right—not like me." Daria quickly drained the rest of her wine. She giggled and toyed with the glass. "I must have dated every guy in the Pit, and slept with half of them." She motioned with her head to the women in the room. "Most of these girls are in the same boat—they didn't stay with their original guy. After all, take a look." She swept an unsteady hand toward the kitchen. "Where else can you find so many studs in one place? Once you make the mistake of going for someone else, you're passed around Alpha Base like a piece of meat."

Vikki felt a pang of sorrow for her. She tried to squash the feeling, embarrassed at her empathy. "Surely everyone's not in the same situation."

Daria's voice was bitter. "Why do you think we're not mixing with the women in the kitchen? Or in the other room? The 'truly faithful' are clinging to their men. Like you should be, dear."

Vikki made up her mind. If she was going to pull this off, she couldn't afford to be seen mingling with Daria's crowd—it wouldn't do to have George Britnell's suspicion's raised.

Vikki smiled sweetly and handed her drink to Daria. "Thanks for the advice, *dear.*"

Daria blinked. "Good luck. You'll need it."

Vikki stopped before leaving, her curiosity getting the best of her. "By the way, if you've been passed around Alpha Base, then why are you staying? Why don't you find another crowd?"

Daria looked shocked. "And miss a chance to nail one of these guys? You'll find out—once you've tasted steak, it's hard to get excited about hamburger."

Vikki just smiled and headed for the kitchen. Spotting Britnell, she moved next to him and slipped an arm around his waist. He patted her hand and didn't even look up.

7

Wednesday, 8 June, 1500 local

Wendover AFB, Utah

McGriffin wound his way past the flight line. His 'vette was fourteen years old, but it handled like new. It was his cadet car—bought during his Firstie, or senior year, at the Academy. Since only first classmen were allowed cars, the 'vette remained special. He turned off the air conditioner and rolled down his window, allowing the dry desert heat to roll in. The air contained a potpourri of JP-4 and engine exhaust. The smell took getting used to, but McGriffin was addicted to it. Like a hearty stout, the fragrance of flying was acquired.

An ancient HH-53 roared overhead, its blades chopping at the air as it turned for the desert. A few miles to the north a flight of helicopters circled lazily, momentarily touching down in the desert on a pickup exercise. Across the runway a deserted hangar reflected the sun back into his eyes.

Once past the flight line, the road dog-eared to the north, then back west, as it headed out to Alpha Base. At the end of the runway a camouflaged C-141B sat on the concrete apron. Red engine protectors sealed the engine inlets from the dust and wind. A series of lights surrounded the apron, glowing dimly in the bright sunlight.

The road to Alpha Base was an anomaly. McGriffin thought that after building the world's most advanced nuclear storage area, they would have spent a small percentage of the total funds on a decent road. Instead, the two-lane road wound around the desert as if designed by a drunk.

The mammoth crater opened up before him. Five miles across and half a mile deep, the crater had a dirt floor with bunkers spread randomly throughout the area.

He tried to count the bunkers, but quickly lost interest as more and more of the concrete shelters came into view. Four fences curled around the area, clearly demarcating the storage facility from the rest of the base.

It seemed barren, almost as if he were alone out there; but after last night's display of readiness, McGriffin shuddered to think what would happen if anyone would be crazy enough to try and get through the fences.

As he turned into the Alpha Base parking lot, he glanced at his watch: 1500. If the tour took any longer than an hour, it was AAFES burgers for dinner again.

He positioned his cap before climbing from the car. A huge sign directed him toward a building marked IN-PROCESSING. Set partially inside the fenced area, it appeared to be the only entrance to Alpha Base besides the main gate.

A young officer stood when McGriffin entered the building. Decked out in smartly pressed battle fatigues, subdued insignia, and bloused boots, the man extended a mammoth ebony hand.

"Good afternoon, sir. I'm Lieutenant Curtis Felowmate, shift commander." Felowmate wore an infectious grin. Towering over McGriffin, he seemed the type to ride herd on a few hundred enlisted men.

"Glad to meet you, Lieutenant. Thanks for arranging the tour on such short notice."

"No problem, sir. Chief Zolley twixted your clearance over. As soon as we've run you through the wringer, we'll get you down in the Pit."

"The wringer?"

Felowmate swung the door open. A small, featureless room lay inside. "You'll find out. When you're in the room, just do what you're told, sir. I'll meet you on the other side."

McGriffin straightened his shoulders and walked into the chamber. As the door clicked shut behind him, McGriffin noticed a mirror on one of the walls. A panel slid open directly under the mirror. One-way mirror, McGriffin thought. Nothing too unusual yet.

A disembodied voice came from the panel. "Step up to the panel and look into the mirror." McGriffin stared, as directed. A moment passed, then the voice announced, "Please step to your left.

A door slid open, opposite from the direction he'd entered. Stepping out into a vacant hallway, McGriffin waited for Felowmate.

A moment passed before the lieutenant strode into the hall. "Ready, sir?"

McGriffin frowned. "That's it?"

"Here." Felowmate led him into a small vestibule

set off to the side. A security policeman nodded as they entered. Looking around, McGriffin spotted the one-way mirror and stared into the tiny room he had been locked in.

Felowmate pointed to several digital readouts. "When you entered the room, your weight was recorded from scales set into the floor." He patted a telescopic object jutting close to the mirror. "This is an optical sensor that recorded your retina pattern and compared it to the digitized pattern that Chief Zolley sent over with your clearance. In addition, an ultrasound was made to see what you carried on your person. If we suspect that you aren't who you're supposed to be, the room seals off and we send in an armed team to drag you out and *really* question you."

McGriffin whistled. "I'll say. No wonder you call this the wringer."

"We normally serve seven-day shifts at Alpha Base, so we have to go through the wringer only once a week. And except for a team that patrols outside Alpha Base, no one enters or leaves during the week. Actually, it's a lot faster than having guards strip-search us."

Leaving the vestibule, they reached an outside door. Sunshine flooded through the window, heating the floor where the light fell. McGriffin hesitated before going outside. "Go ahead, Major. Once you passed through the wringer, you were officially inside Alpha Base." He opened the door for McGriffin. As they stepped outside, Felowmate pointed out a heavily guarded gate. Barbed and razor wire covered the entrance. A tunnel of empty space two hundred feet deep, fifty feet high, and one hundred feet across was carved into the wire.

"That's the only other way to get in or out of Alpha Base. We only use it when we're moving nuclear weapons. When it's open, Alpha Base is put on alert."

McGriffin squinted at the gate to where the four fences came together. At the intersection, razor wire rose in an intricate three-dimensional mesh. The tunnel was large enough to accommodate the flatbeds carrying nuclear weapons. The gates on either side of the tunnel were never open simultaneously.

McGriffin picked out a few of the other landmarks. A low building marked ALPHA BASE COMMAND POST/RED ROOM stood next to two other buildings: ENLISTED BARRACKS and OFFICERS' QUARTERS. The enlisted barracks were ten times bigger than the officers' quarters. That made sense—there should be at least a ten-to-one ratio of enlisted to officer here.

Felowmate tugged on McGriffin's elbow. "I'll take you on a quick tour of the area before we go to the command post."

They climbed into a jeep marked COMMAND SECTION. As McGriffin buckled in, Felowmate reached down and flipped a switch. "IFF—Identification Friend or Foe," he explained. "We track every object within a radius of five miles of Alpha Base on radar unless they have one of these IFF devices. That's classified confidential, by the way, Major. If we didn't have the IFF's, we'd be going crazy tracking all of the security vehicles."

"So you were able to track my car?"

"That's one advantage to working out here. We can't be caught in a surprise inspection—we always have plenty of warning for anything that comes our way. A computer automatically masks out any blips from an IFF source, effectively making the image invisible to radar."

As they started off, McGriffin shook his head. "It's nice that you have IFF's that work. They're different from the ones I've used when flying; I wouldn't use one of our IFF's in this place if you paid me."

"How's that?" yelled Felowmate.

McGriffin leaned toward Felowmate so the lieutenant could hear him over the engine. "I have an Army buddy who works in a Hawk unit—you know, the ones that provide anti-air support for the ground troops? They're supposed to use the IFF's to tell the good guys from the bad guys in a war. Well, this guy says they're so unreliable, they're going to go ahead and shoot at anything that flies over their Hawk sites."

"So what do you pilots think about that?"

"That's why I'm a trash hauler and not a fighter pilot—I *don't* worry about it."

Felowmate patted the IFF. "Well, these are state-of-the-art, and we haven't had any problems with them. Not yet, anyway."

He slowed the jeep as they drove up to a bunker. The bunker was unguarded, but it looked formidable. They climbed out and walked toward the bulwark. A concrete driveway led up to the bunker. A searchlight, shielded with a grid of steel, sat on top of the concrete wall. The bunker's face jutted out from a mound of dirt. Felowmate placed a hand on the steel door as McGriffin poked around the exterior.

"The door's made of four-inch-thick steel, originally manufactured as siding for battleships. The concrete walls are eight feet thick, reinforced with rebar, and built to survive a direct hit by a twenty-thousand-pound bomb."

"How do you open it?" McGriffin pounded on the steel. It didn't vibrate or budge to his blow.

Felowmate motioned him over to a small steel box embedded in the bunker's side. He leaned against the box. "We've gone to a holographic keying system. It's impossible to break into."

McGriffin lifted his brows. "Impossible?"

"There's over a billion trillion possible combinations available from the interference patterns in the holograph."

McGriffin whistled. Felowmate swept his arm across the view of the crater. "We have the capability of storing most of the nation's stockpile of nuclear weapons here. And that's what the Department of Defense is heading toward. I guess they want to save money by consolidating the storage sites; that, and keeping the Russkies happy."

McGriffin leaned against the steel door and gazed across the expanse of Alpha Base. It seemed so calm. The sand was quiet, undisturbed by even the presence of insects. A slight chopping from unseen helicopters was barely audible. If not for the presence of the bunkers and ubiquitous four fences, the scene would have been straight out of a John Wayne western.

McGriffin put a hand in his pocket. "Do you think it's a good idea to have the entire national stockpile under one roof?"

Lieutenant Felowmate looked startled. "Huh? I don't know. I mean, I'm just a lieutenant, not a general. I've never thought about that."

"Well, what do you think?" pressed McGriffin.

"You saw the guards. Even the air space around Alpha Base is restricted. We've got RAIDS—that's a Radar Airborne Intrusion Detection System—coupled with anti-aircraft missiles using Passive Optical Sensing Technology. The POST Stingers have orders to shoot down anything that flies overhead."

"Isn't that a little radical?"

Felowmate looked grim. "We're at the top of all *Notes to Airmen*. We have a five-mile buffer zone with searchlights, radio warnings, and flares to wave off planes if they get close. If they keep heading for us . . ." He shrugged.

A warm gust of wind whipped around the two,

kicking up sand. McGriffin glanced at his watch. "Sounds like you play hardball, Lieutenant."

"We're dead serious, sir."

"I guess that answers my question about a single repository." They turned and headed back down into the crater to the jeep. "I was just a little concerned last night when that rabbit made it through two of your fences."

"On the contrary, sir, if a rabbit can't get through our defenses, then nothing can."

McGriffin glanced at his watch again. "I appreciate the time you've spent, but my shift at the base command post begins in a little over an hour and a half. Do you mind if I get back to you on that tour of your command post?"

"I think the Red Room would be more interesting —it's where we keep our nuke mock-ups, kind of a show-and-tell. Do you have your CNWDI clearance yet?"

McGriffin frowned, then remembered that CNWDI stood for Critical Nuclear Weapons Design Information. "Yeah. I was briefed into it yesterday." McGriffin climbed into the jeep. "Maybe you guys can throw some excitement back into my life."

Felowmate started the engine. He popped the vehicle into gear and they lurched off. "If you're into rabbits, then you've already experienced all the excitement you'll see."

As they drove back in silence, McGriffin hoped that Felowmate was right.

The sheet fell away from her breast as she rolled over to her side. She placed a hand on his chest.

Britnell started giggling, then laughed as she rolled on top of him.

He pulled her down and they kissed. She propped

her head up on an elbow. "We'll have to do this again sometime."

Britnell stretched. "Anything you want, babe. I'll give you the world if you want."

Vikki murmured, "Anything?"

"Yeah. Anything."

She hesitated, then drew a finger across his chest. She really wanted to pull him in, string him along longer . . . but if she asked for something innocuous, she could build up to the important things. "You know, it might help if I could get a hold of a Wendover phone book. I have to go through base information for just about everything. It would really come in handy when we make appointments with your contracting division."

"No problem." He closed his eyes.

Vikki reached over and flicked off the light. She rolled to her side and snuggled up against him, smiling.

8

Thursday, 9 June, 1223 local

Wendover, Nevada

"You'll have to check out the staging area by yourself. I've got to go to Baja."

"Why?" Vikki Osborrn pushed back her hair. "I'm getting close to finding all we want to know about Alpha Base, including the call signs and map. We can't afford to blow it now. Can't you handle it when you get back?"

Anthony Harding stood silent for a moment. He sounded weary. "I have to finalize the plans with this mercenary group that NUFA dug up."

Vikki eyed Harding as he walked across her apartment. An old television sat in one corner, facing a threadbare couch and a coffee table. A card table and three folding chairs made up the rest of the room. Ashtrays held just as much residue from marijuana as est-to-goodness *New Mexican* Mexican food: TexMex from tobacco. The double bed in the bedroom was unmade, and clothes were strewn over boxes.

She raised an eyebrow at Harding. Here she was, prostituting her body, giving herself to Britnell, for a higher cause. The zeal that she and Harding had once felt was gone now, and their lovemaking was replaced with a mechanical, almost predictable, rhythmic grinding.

Britnell's caresses brought back the fervor—but it was tempered with the knowledge that she was no better than some slut on the main strip. It almost made her vomit to go through with it.

But it was that elusive higher law—*the end justifies the means*—that kept her smiling while courting Britnell. Through all his groping, she kept that one goal in mind: she'd put up with anything to get rid of the nukes, or at least be able to prove to the rest of the nation how easy it was to steal one.

And now Harding wanted to go cavorting off and leave *her* to finish his work.

Harding placed his hands on the back of the couch. "You've got to find a landing strip in the mountains, one big enough for a C-130, so it will have to be at least a mile long. You've got to get up there, spend a few days to find what we need. I've . . . I've got to hammer out the assault plans."

"No. If we're going to pull this plan off, *I've* got to keep seeing Britnell. His ego is too fragile. If I leave now, he'll go to pieces. Even for a few days. Can't you do it when you get back?"

Silence. Harding held up his hands. "Britnell can wait."

Vikki bit her lip; she couldn't believe that he was dismissing the whole reason for what she was doing.

She spoke with an edge to her voice. "If we steal those nukes, the U.S. will take so much heat they'll be forced to upgrade security, maybe even get rid of some of their arsenal. If NUFA wants to bring the country to its knees, this is the way to do it. And that means working through Britnell."

"Look, these mercenary clowns are running the assault," Harding snapped. "They can't fly in here unless we find a staging area. *That*'s the key—not Britnell. And they're pretty dammed serious about it, too."

"Screw the mercenaries. If they're threatening you, then they don't really care about the nukes. Remember why we got involved in NUFA: *to get rid of the nukes.* That's the only thing that counts. Let's do what we came to do."

Harding slammed a hand against the wall. They remained silent for some time, staring at each other.

Jumbled thoughts roared through Vikki's mind. The nukes, she thought. There's nothing more important than getting rid of the nukes. If that wasn't true, then she wouldn't be leading Britnell on—having sex with the airhead every moment they were together. Or Harding, as it was turning out. The sacrifices were piling up, but the end in sight seemed smaller, constricting.

Harding spoke with his back to her. He picked up his bags. "Do what you have to. But remember, no staging area, no raid. It's as simple as that. I'm going to Baja."

Wendover AFB, Utah

"So this is a Jolly Green Giant."

The flight-suited man whirled and shot a glance at McGriffin's name tag. "That's right, sir. Actually it's a Super Jolly Green. I'm Captain Manny Yarnez. I'll be taking you up today."

"How do you do, Manny. Bill's the name."

Manny returned McGriffin's handshake with a firm grip. Red-haired and lithe, Manny's infectious grin sparkled. The airman who had escorted McGriffin out to the flight line backed away to the staff car. A flight-suited master sergeant who looked at least five years older than McGriffin walked around the craft, completing a preflight checklist. He nodded to McGriffin as he passed. Manny squinted at McGriffin's pilot wings. "Fixed wing?"

"One forty-one's for thirteen years."

Manny whistled. "Must be nice. We get our share of Starlifters through here."

McGriffin looked wistful. "I've noticed." He started to warm up to the chopper pilot.

Manny motioned for McGriffin to follow him around the craft. He walked behind the master sergeant, quickly looking over the blades and ensuring all panels were closed. Manny reached inside the cockpit and hauled out a flight log. He scanned the names and dates, then nodded to himself. "Looks like we're in luck. She's good for another ten hours."

McGriffin looked along the helicopter's side. The skin looked strange in the sunlight. It was dull black, devoid of any shine. The rotor assembly was encased in the material. Examining the skin closer, he couldn't even see where the sun reflected. He rubbed a finger against the fuselage; the skin was ice cold. "What have you guys painted this with?"

Ducking back around to the opposite side, Manny swung up into the craft. McGriffin hesitated, then followed. Manny said absently, "It's a radar absorber. It cuts our cross section down to almost zero. That and the electronic countermeasure gear add about five hundred pounds to our weight. The drawback is that it also absorbs heat like crazy but doesn't radiate it, so it heats up fast inside. That keeps us from being a sitting duck for infrared sensors, but we lose five pounds from sweating every time we fly." He motioned for McGriffin to climb into the jump seat behind the pilot's seat. Strapping himself in, he turned and grinned back at McGriffin.

"They're adding all kinds of bells-and-whistles to our birds. I guess they've forgotten we're supposed to be rescue. They tried to redesignate us as SH-53's, but we nearly revolted: if they wanted stealth capability, they should have bought some more B-2's and left us alone. But that's politics for you." He scanned flight line. "As soon as Lieutenant Nederden gets out here, we'll be ready to blast off."

McGriffin leaned forward in his seat. "Sorry about the short notice. I'm trying to hit most of the units on base while I still have some free time."

"S'all right. Have you been up yet?"

"Not here. I have a private pilot's license, but haven't gotten a chance to check out a plane. In fact, that sounds like a good idea. I'd appreciate you showing me around the whole base."

"Good. We'll give you the VIP tour then. Just sit back and enjoy."

A young lieutenant climbed on board, interrupting Manny. Manny shot a glance over his shoulder. "You ready, Bill?" Manny didn't wait for McGriffin's answer. Flicking on his mike, he gave a thumbs-up to the master sergeant in the rear of the craft. The flight engineer flipped on the helicopter's auxiliary power unit; a whine split the air. Manny turned; he had a twinkle in his eye. "Let me know if you get airsick."

McGriffin snorted. *Me? Airsick in a helicopter?* He was going to like this guy.

Friday, 10 June, 0925 local

Baja, Mexico

The ocean was five miles away, but Harding could hear the waves crashing against the craggy coastline. Humidity permeated the air. The dirt landing strip ran past the Cessna, stretching out until it ended in a jumble of rocks. The sky was cloudless, and the blueness was so deep it reminded Harding of the flight down here when he looked out the window and saw the Gulf of California stretching out below. Miles above any pollution, when he looked up he had felt as if he could see the stars.

It was a wild jumble of sunshine, desert rocks, shimmering heat, and ocean. Baja was an untamed paradise.

Harding stood by the single-engine airplane that had flown him from Orange County's John Wayne Airport. A helicopter and two small planes were secured at the opposite end of the runway. A large four-engine plane, painted solid black, sat fifty yards away. It was a military transport, but it bore no identifying markings. Harding couldn't place the model, but it looked like a C-130.

To his left stood a mock-up of an Alpha Base storage bunker. Tin siding substituted for concrete walls, but the effect was the same: it presented a monolithic fortress to conquer.

A set of four fences ran on the other side of the bunker. The facility was not to scale, but it gave the terrorists something to practice with.

The terrorists were alone, the nearest people tens of miles away. Do'brainese guards ensured their privacy, driving back approaching fishermen and enterprising four-wheelers from up north.

Standing in front of Harding, General Ashtah looked resplendent in his Do'brainese uniform: gold piping, flashy ribbons, jaunty cap. Harding snorted; the general also looked like a tin soldier. Old and wheezing, the officer acted as if he were in the midst of his last hurrah.

A group of fifty men lounged behind the general, eating assorted fruits and laughing quietly among themselves. They sprawled over rusting jeeps. A few managed to find some shade under the aircraft's wing. For the most part they seemed content to rest instead of work. A few pointed comments drifted from the group.

One man stood apart from the others. Erect and impeccably dressed in a creased khaki uniform, the man appeared to be the real leader of the group; he carried himself differently from the Do'brainese general who now had Harding's attention.

Harding recalled the Do'brai connection that had brought him here: in a daring attempt to kidnap the President of the U.S. and force America's hand for supporting Third World demands, Do'brai had lost face when the kidnapping had failed. An American rescue mission had not only brought back the President, but had also brought back the Do'brainese general responsible for planning the coup. No wonder these guys want revenge, Harding thought. And they couldn't have picked anyone better than me to pull this together.

Harding smiled and said, "General Ashtah, my associate, Vikki Osborrn, has been instrumental in our effort to gain entry into Alpha Base. She has gained the confidence of one of the guards, and he has brought her into his circle of friends."

General Ashtah removed his cap and wiped at his brow with a handkerchief. He smiled crookedly and spoke excellent English. "Yes, Vikki is playing a very important role."

"This is not a game, General."

"No, it is not. But nevertheless, I wanted your personal assurance that this operation will not fail."

"It won't. There is too much at stake."

"Ah, yes," said General Ashtah slowly. He swiped at his brow. "And if something goes wrong—"

"I said it *won't,*" interrupted Harding.

"It always does," said Ashtah gently. He put his cap back on and motioned with his hand. "Here, let us walk and enjoy the view."

Harding and Ashtah walked abreast of each other. The general strolled with his hands in his pockets. They walked away from the crude runway toward a field of boulders. Once out of range of the men, General Ashtah toed a rock. "Have you ever been to the Baja peninsula, Dr. Harding?"

"No."

The general bent over and picked up the rock. He

turned it over in his hand. "It is a beautiful place. Sunny, desolate—it is almost like my home of Do'brai, except for this humidity." He pulled out his handkerchief and wiped at his brow. "The Mexican government has given us permission to use this little spot with no strings attached."

Harding looked impatient. "What's your point?"

The general eyed a boulder and tossed his rock at it. The stone missed, then careened off another boulder. He wiped his hands and turned back to Harding. "My homeland was invaded by an American force not long ago. The event was not publicized, but we lost a great deal of face that day—as well as one of our generals."

Ashtah waved his arm at the collection of men. "When I turn over Colonel Renault and his men to you, we are making a commitment to bring the U.S. to its knees for what it did to us. We could not do this without your help—and you cannot proceed without ours. It places us in a very vulnerable situation, Dr. Harding. If we are discovered, we may be invaded again, and this time for keeps . . ." His voice trailed off.

Harding brushed away tiny beads of perspiration forming on his brow. "My country is committing a crime against humanity, stockpiling these nuclear weapons. Anything I can do to prevent the United States from having them is well worth my life."

"Your life may depend on it, Dr. Harding."

"I realize that."

"And so may the life of this Vikki Osborrn."

Harding hesitated. "Vikki is not aware of Do'brai's involvement in this operation. The only reason she is participating in the raid is to increase security at Alpha Base, to show how easy it is to steal a nuke, and perhaps to have the U.S. reduce its number of nuclear weapons. She believes this is purely a NUFA-backed operation. She is very idealistic . . ."

General Ashtah raised an eyebrow. "I do not want idealism to get in the way of practicality."

Harding set his mouth. "She is idealistic, but necessary to the plan. But on the other hand, *no one* is expendable. If she gets in the way . . ." He shrugged.

A warm gust blew past, sending the general's hat sailing. He grabbed at it and juggled it until he had a good grasp. "Very well, Dr. Harding. I am glad we had this meeting. I appreciate your sincerity."

"And I appreciate yours, General."

General Ashtah turned smartly and strode briskly to the military transport. Harding followed at his heels.

The group of men sprang to attention when Ashtah approached. He spoke sharply to them in an incomprehensible language. When he stopped, the men cheered. Ashtah turned and nodded to Harding before commandeering a jeep and driving away.

Harding walked toward the men. They formed a ragged semicircle in front of him. One man, the man who appeared to be in charge, stepped forward. He took a deep drag on a cigarette and threw it to the ground. "I'm Macklin Renault, in charge of this unit. General Ashtah said that you'll brief us about Alpha Base."

Harding looked puzzled as he shook Renault's hand. "Mr. Renault, I thought the Do'brainese militia would assist us."

Renault smiled wearily. His blond hair contrasted with a deep tan, his eyes steady, unwavering, as they seemed to take in every detail. "Perhaps I should have introduced myself as *Colonel* Renault, Doctor. My men are commissioned in Do'brai's army."

"But you're obviously not Do'brainese . . ."

Renault spoke softly. "Does it matter, Dr. Harding? The French have fought their wars for years like this. I hesitate to call us mercenaries—it's such a strong word—but it's fairly descriptive."

Harding raised his brows. "I don't think it matters where you're from, Colonel. As long as I have your allegiance."

"No problem with that. That's what we're getting paid for. My men swear their allegiance to me; they come from all nations and are bound to none. *My* orders are to obey your instructions. Now, I think you had better fill us in on Alpha Base." He steered them away from the men, toward the military transport.

"Just a minute." Harding went back to the Cessna and grabbed a satchel. He lugged the brown bag to Renault. Clearing a place underneath one of the military transport's wings, Harding pulled out a handful of U.S. Park Service maps. Kneeling in the dirt, they pored over them.

Renault pointed at one of the maps. "The crucial item is a staging area for the C-130, away from the public eye but close enough for a helicopter to fly in from Alpha Base."

Harding turned red, remembering the fuss that Vikki had made. "We're taking care of that. But what about your men? Who are the key players?"

Renault stood and nodded to his legion of mercenaries. "I've known these men for years. Some of them are like my own sons." He searched the men's faces for a moment, then pointed. "There, Frank Helenmotz, the sandy-haired man sitting by the runway . . . and over there, Pablo Jaqueratee, the Jamaican by the mock-up bunker. Those are two of my best."

Harding stood, wiping his hands on his pants. He

73

squinted at the man called Helenmotz; the man sat alone and chewed on a fingernail, silently looking out over the runway.

Renault said, "Helenmotz was born too late for 'Nam. He joined the Army when he was seventeen and tried to get into Airborne. They refused him a chance for his third jump after he decked the Airborne chaplain, so he put in for helicopter training.

"The Army felt that it had to give people a second chance. So instead of a court-martial, he went to Fort Rucker, flying choppers. But at Rucker he decked his flight instructor after a shouting match on the tarmac, something about Helenmotz sleeping with the instructor's wife. That time they booted him out of the Army. Now he flies for me."

Renault nodded next to the Jamaican. Tall and lanky, Pablo Jaqueratee tossed a small ball around with a group of men. Renault said, "Pablo joined me five years ago. I needed a guard to direct an arms shipment in—Pablo held ten flares in a row, keeping them until the flame burned down to his fingers, the last smoldering his flesh so he couldn't open his hand. But the shipment got through, all because of him."

Renault turned at Harding. "He'll do anything, and won't quit while he's at it. The same goes for Helenmotz."

Harding stretched his legs. He said, "Okay, sounds good. But what about the two hundred guards on Alpha Base? Can your men really take out the barracks?"

Renault narrowed his eyes. "We've got it down to a science, Dr. Harding. Watch." He turned and snapped an order in Spanish. One of his men jumped up and dragged a mortar in front of Harding.

Renault pointed to a shack, hundreds of yards away.

Kneeling, the man took a sighting and adjusted the weapon. He looked up. At Renault's nod, he dropped a round into the mortar. A blast erupted from the device. Seconds later the shack exploded in a ball of flames.

Harding's eyes widened. "Impressive."

Looking back at the map Renault said, "Dr. Harding—I think we've got a plan. My men will go over several variations of this and come up with something we're comfortable with. The key is to attack Alpha Base when they're least expecting it. In the meantime, if you can iron out things on your end, I think one more meeting should do it."

"Good." Harding vigorously shook his hand. "We'll have the landing strip and moving van ready this week."

"My men can move out with a few hours notice." Renault held out his hand. "What about the call signs and map? If we're going to do this right under their noses, we have to have the proper clearance to land at Wendover."

"That shouldn't be a problem. Vikki—the woman working with me—is obtaining a detailed map of Alpha Base as well as the correct call signs." Harding shook Renault's hand. "I'll fly down later in the week and accompany you to the staging area. Vikki will be in position to give us a go when everything is ready."

"Good. That leaves one final thing. Can you get hold of an IFF?" At Harding's puzzled look, Renault said, "Don't worry about what it means. If Vikki can get one, then fine. Otherwise, we'll have to drive right up to Alpha Base."

Harding nodded. "We'll work on it."

"Great. Good luck."

They shook hands and departed. As Harding left,

Renault commandeered his men into a semicircle around him. Renault pointed to various points around the four fences and mock-up of Alpha Base.

The Cessna rocked slightly when Harding climbed inside. He slammed the door and shimmied into the right seat, next to the pilot. The plane's engine sputtered as it caught, revving up to maximum power.

The plane bounced a few times as it sped down the dirt runway. The sensation was almost gut-wrenching as the small craft finally hopped into the air. They climbed in altitude as they banked away from the peninsula.

The plane suddenly dove low, reaching for the valleys in between the northern Mexican terrain as it attempted to elude American border patrols. Pressed into service for drug interdiction, the Navy's E-2 radar planes could spot them if they flew too high. The craft bounced in the thermals. Harding's stomach flipped with every bump. But it was nothing compared to what was to come.

Salt Lake City, Utah

The man grinned at Vikki. He spread his elbows out over the counter and picked at his teeth. "Now, let me get this straight. You want this moving van for two weeks?"

"That's right."

"And you're going to deliver it back here?"

"What's so unusual about that?" Vikki grew impatient.

The man straightened. The lot behind him overflowed with various-size trucks, everything from pickups to thirty-two-foot-long vans. Dirt piled up in a corner of the office. A board holding the vehicle keys was full. He pushed a set of papers across the counter.

"Look, lady. Most people are either moving in or out of Salt Lake—no one rents a moving van for two weeks and doesn't leave town."

Vikki scribbled her name on the sheet and looked up heatedly. "It's none of your damned business, but if you have to know, my girlfriend and I are taking our time moving to a new apartment." She pushed back her hair. It was hard enough dealing with this clown, especially after Harding had come back, making more demands on her time with IFF's and other nonsense.

The man's grin widened. "You know, if you need any help—"

"We don't." Vikki pushed the papers back to the man. She pulled out a wad of bills and shoved them toward him, too. "That should cover it."

The man shrugged. Turning, he picked off one of the keys from the board and handed it to her. "You've got the first twenty-four-footer on the lot. It's the one with the cabin over the driver's seat. It's due back the week after Wednesday, three o'clock sharp. Bring it back with a full tank of gas."

Vikki swept up the key and turned to leave. The man called after her, "Don't forget to double-clutch in low gear." Vikki ignored him and headed for the moving van.

9

Monday, 13 June, 1400 local

Wendover AFB, Utah

With six hours of sleep under his belt, McGriffin felt better than he had in months. Well, weeks at least. His command post schedule was reminiscent of flying Military Air Command hops across the pond.

For some unknown reason, MAC aircraft couldn't take off at a decent hour. It had to be one in the morning, or some such nonsense. That first year he flew 141's, he didn't know the sun shined at most of the bases he flew into.

McGriffin was feeling reckless, so he decided to pass up the usual trip to the AAFES grill and splurge on some real food downtown. Earlier, a quick jaunt in a Cessna at the aero club qualified him for flying the club's airplanes. If the gusts hadn't been so bad, he'd have stayed up longer.

For the second time since he'd arrived at Wendover,

he decided to use what little free time he had and run into town; the first had been a disappointing jaunt to check out the local churches—aside from the usual "grip-and-grin" snake-oil salesmen masquerading as Christians, he hadn't been able to find a true Bible-teaching congregation. It was going to be a long tour.

Before leaving the Bachelor Officer Quarters, he rinsed out his hair and allowed his locks to fly. After Colonel DeVries's pointed comments, he was careful to keep his hair looking short by plastering it to his head. But he didn't have to keep it slicked down if he wasn't in uniform. Looking like a civilian, he finally felt human again.

The view off Interstate 80 was breathtaking. Situated just outside Wendover, Nevada, several observation towers stood by the highway, allowing tourists to take in the scenery. Standing in one of the towers, white sand stretched as far as he could see. In the distance the heat rose as a shimmering wave, making the ground appear as if it were submerged.

The warmth felt good. Even though he had fallen in love with Tacoma, the wet rain chilled him and he had never seemed able to shake it. But now the warmth permeated his bones. Along with the dry air, he felt as if he could never leave the desert. Realizing he'd been holding his breath, he let out a lungful of air.

"It takes your breath away, doesn't it?"

"Yeah." McGriffin turned. The woman was stunning. Long blond hair hung straight down. She didn't wear any makeup; rounded breasts pleasantly filled her blouse. McGriffin turned back to the railing. He hadn't heard her approach.

The woman joined him, propping her elbows up on the metal railing. They were shielded from the sun, but the sun's reflection still made them squint. The woman flipped her hair back over a shoulder.

"It's so white. The sand seems unreal," she said.

McGriffin pointed to where the sand ran up against the mountains. "It makes the mountains look purple."

She squinted to where he pointed. "You're right." The woman turned and leaned back against the railing. She studied him and folded her arms. "You a local?"

"I've been here for about a week. Just moved into town."

"So did I."

Her voice had a slight bite to it—almost as if she were hardened against something. But she seemed pleasant enough.

She turned and leaned on the railing. A breeze made her hair fly. "It sure is beautiful."

"If you think this is pretty, you ought to see it from the air."

"You a pilot?"

"Yeah. I fly a little." Not nearly as much as I'd like, he thought. He didn't expound. He didn't know how people reacted to the military presence around here yet. Some people were funny about finding out he was in the Air Force—his longish hair usually hid the fact. He changed the subject by motioning with his head to an old woman running a snack stand. "Thirsty?" The woman furrowed her brows as if in deep thought. McGriffin waited a moment, then said, "You're not going anywhere, are you? Come on, how about a pop?"

She suddenly brightened. "Sure, why not? I've got time."

McGriffin dug out a bill and paid for both drinks over her protests.

She drained half the soft drink before putting it

down. McGriffin sipped his as she wiped at her mouth. She said, "I didn't realize I was that thirsty."

"The humidity is so low, your perspiration evaporates nearly as fast as it's formed. It's easy to overheat and not know it." McGriffin caught himself. "Sorry. I didn't mean to lecture. I—"

"No, it's all right. Really." She sipped at her drink. "I've been here about a week, and I haven't taken time to learn anything about Wendover. You know, do the tourist thing."

"I lived in Washington State for almost two years before getting out and seeing the area." And that was only because of the divorce, thought McGriffin.

The woman thought for a moment. "You know, I did about the same thing. Lived in the Bay Area for years and never really saw that much."

They were silent for some minutes while they finished their drinks. McGriffin stole a few glances at her before tossing his container in the trash. He glanced at his watch. *Command post in two hours.* "Well, I'd probably better be going. It was nice meeting you." He stopped, stymied over what to say next.

She stuck out her hand. "I'm Vikki Osborrn. Glad to meet you."

"Bill McGriffin. Uh, maybe I can buy you another drink sometime?"

She brushed back her hair. "Sure. I'd like that."

McGriffin patted his pockets and pulled out a pen. "I could give you a call."

She hesitated; then, "Sure." She scribbled a number and gave the paper back to him. "I'm free most days before five."

"Great." McGriffin backed up as he was leaving. "Great, I'll call. Great." He almost stumbled over a trash can on his way out.

Tuesday, 14 June, 1920 local

Wendover, Nevada

"Who was it?"

"Nobody important." Vikki put down the phone and smiled at Britnell. He unsteadily drained his fifth beer and bleared at her.

"Then who are you meeting at noon tomorrow? I heard you make an appointment."

Vikki slid up to the young airman and gave him a peck on the cheek. He wasn't as drunk as she had thought. "Some guy at the airport. I'm looking into taking flying lessons." Britnell grunted and pushed her backward on the bed.

Vikki ran her hands across his shoulders. "I'm really going to miss you when you go out to the Pit. I wish I could see you."

Britnell seemed jolted, as if his week-long stay coming up at Alpha Base were a revelation to him. "There's a way to get around it. Ever hear of an Identification Friend or Foe, an IFF?" His words were slurred.

Vikki grew alert. "Hmmm?"

"Well, I've got one on my Bronco. I might be able to get away for a while—the IFF will mask us. You don't have to wait a week for me to get off duty."

"Sounds fascinating." She didn't want to seem too eager; besides, she'd be able to pull more out of him when he was coherent. "George."

"Uh?"

82

"That construction contract, the one my company is bidding for?"

"Yeah—what about it?"

"Is there any way you could get me an area map of the Pit? That's the last bit of information we need. If we knew where the service lines were located, we could bid a bigger building for the new barracks."

"New barracks?" He thought for a moment, blinking. "Sure, that's no problem. The place is a rat hole now."

"Don't say anything about this—they might think you're giving us an unfair advantage in the competition."

"There's no competing with you, babe."

Vikki closed her eyes. She tried not to grimace. Britnell moved on top of her, roughly.

The motions seemed to come mechanically. She bit her lip and stole a quick glance at her watch. *Five minutes.* The erotic rapture had fled, leaving only garlic from dinner and beer-laced sweat from coupling. Another few minutes and he'd be through—either hopelessly spent, or too drunk to continue the sex.

It was coupling, executed in dull, automated fashion.

Vikki turned her head and looked at the telephone.

10

Alpha Base

Major McGriffin presented his ID card to the guard and refrained from whistling. The guard checked McGriffin's name against a computerized roster. The young airman sternly flipped the card over, then handed it back to McGriffin. After the wringer, the security measures in the Red Room seemed a piece of cake. Located inside Alpha Base's command post, the Red Room's door wasn't even painted red.

The tour was his last for a while. The plethora of facts tired him—in some ways it was like taking a drink of water from a fire hose. The information piled up. Most of it was interesting, but he had neither the time nor the memory to digest all the details.

But again, it kept his mind off Linda. And anything that did that *had* to be good for him.

McGriffin glanced at his watch. He was early, and

Lieutenant Felowmate was nowhere in sight. The husky lieutenant had been a godsend, volunteering his time to show him the ropes. Usually the nonrated officers kept their distance from the rated types. It was some kind of ego problem in reverse.

But McGriffin didn't attribute Lieutenant Felowmate's friendliness completely to the fact that they were both Academy grads. McGriffin sincerely thought that the young man would have taken the same pains with anyone in McGriffin's position.

Felowmate appeared, breaking his train of thought. "How do you do, Major?"

"Great. I appreciate the time you're spending, Curtis."

"Like I said, no problem. The more you know about our facility and what we keep here, the better we can do our job."

"You still sound reluctant to admit you store nuclear weapons."

Felowmate cringed. "Matter of habit, sir. You know, official Air Force policy: we're supposed to neither confirm nor deny the existence of any nuclear devices."

"Nuclear devices. You make it sound so sanitary."

Felowmate laughed. "If I remember, you've got command post at 1800. I'll try to keep the time down."

At the end of the corridor they approached a vault set into the wall. It resembled a huge safe. Felowmate stopped before the vault and spun the dials.

McGriffin studied a sign by the vault:

THE USE OF PHOTOGRAPHY EQUIPMENT, CAMERAS, ELECTRONIC RECORDING, THE TAKING OF NOTES, OR ANY OTHER REPRODUCIBLE MEDIA **IS**

STRICTLY PROHIBITED.
PLEASE SECURE THE DOOR BEHIND YOU.

Stepping over the steel rim jutting up from the floor, they entered the vault. Felowmate pulled the portal shut behind them. The huge metal door hissed closed.

McGriffin gaped at the chamber. It was as if thirty thousand square feet of material had been stuffed in a room ten times smaller.

Four tables, each fifty feet long, made up the perimeter of a giant rectangle. At crammed intervals along the table he saw mock-ups of disassembled warheads. Inside the tables were giant "busses," the delivery platforms where the warheads would sit. The room was split up into four distinct sections labeled: 1945–60, 1961–75, 1976–90, 1991–present. Various warheads, triggering devices, delivery vehicles, and even a computerized display of the warhead development phase were all packed into the room.

Felowmate led him around the table. "The displays are roughly grouped by generation. As a rule of thumb, each generation signifies a tenfold increase in weapon efficiency, accuracy, and design. The weapons from the fifties are quite a bit different from those produced in the nineties."

McGriffin whistled and moved around the displays. He stopped before a huge metal container and ran his hand over the surface. A sign above the device read LITTLE BOY—the first nuke ever dropped in a war. And the MARK 17—the first thermonuclear device. The weapon was immense. To think that an ancient B-47 could even carry it was mind-boggling.

Farther down the line a suitcase-size hydrogen weapon looked sleek and succinct compared with the forties-vintage device. Labels such as "Earth/Ice Penetrator," "Howitzer Qualified," "Enhanced Neutron

Radiator," and "B-81" adorned the cramped displays. The inner workings of each device were visible as a slice through the weapon's center.

McGriffin inspected one of the casings. "They made a big deal once about some college student who discovered how to build one of these. My junior high science teacher had us design one for a physics project."

Felowmate lifted an eyebrow. "Junior high?"

"Sure. You slap two pieces of fissionable material together, such as Uranium 235. When enough uranium comes together, a chain reaction occurs, and *blooey*, you've ruined everybody's day. To build a hydrogen bomb, you use the energy from an atomic bomb to compress hydrogen. A fusion reaction occurs, and you've *really* made one big parking lot."

McGriffin stepped back and folded his arms. He took in the chamber and assorted weaponry. "You know, if I could do it in seventh grade, why are people so paranoid about the secrets getting out?"

"The trick is putting the right quantity of material together, with the right timing and symmetry. Refining those quantities, and keeping that knowledge secret is what's critical. Can you imagine what would happen if a few lunatics got a hold of a nuclear device? The nukes all have Permissive Actions Links—PALS —to prevent them from being detonated if they're stolen, plus a host of other things. But still . . ." He trailed off.

McGriffin started to pat the casing, but thought better of it. He glanced at Felowmate, who watched him, grinning.

"These are mock-ups. Besides, you could take a sledgehammer to one of those weapons, Major, and you wouldn't set it off—it's called a one-point design. It can detonate only if a certain timing sequence is initiated. They use a high explosive, something like TNT but a lot more stable, to slap the radioactive material together. The high explosive initiates the implosion.

"They've hurled those warheads against the ground at hundreds of miles an hour, shot at them, put them in fires, set off high explosives next to them—in fact, done just about everything possible, and they *still* don't detonate. That's one thing I've got to say about the failsafe measures that the Department of Energy put into them: it's almost impossible to set one off accidentally."

McGriffin nodded. He surveyed the room. It was another room full of facts, but he felt he had gleaned the salient points from the tour. It was a knack he had picked up as a cadet. He had never cracked a book, but he paid attention in class. Just by listening and taking notes, he was able to maintain a high B average. It had taken him through four years of grief, and he developed a way to quickly grasp what was important. He never knew when any of the information he digested might come in handy.

As he turned to leave the vault, he pulled his hand away from the warhead. Mock-up or not, he still played it safe.

Thursday, 16 June, 1205 local

Wendover AFB, Utah

"Sorry I'm late." McGriffin jumped out of his Corvette and shut the door behind him. "I overslept."

Vikki brushed back her hair, smiling. "It's five minutes after. It must have been some wild party for you to sleep this late." A plane roared overhead, drowning out McGriffin's reply.

He led her into the aero club hanger. He raised his voice over another plane that just started its engines. "Actually, I work nights. It's tough trying to catch up on sleep during the day—especially when it's so nice outside." Opening the door for her, they stepped into an air-conditioned room. "Ever fly in a light plane before?"

She hesitated slightly. "Only once."

McGriffin picked up a pen and started filling out the aero club's rental papers. "What did you think of it?"

"I don't know. I guess I didn't really care for it; it was awfully bumpy."

McGriffin didn't look up. "Probably hit a patch of thermals. Afternoons are notorious for that: the ground heats up the air, and the hot air rises." He pushed the papers across the counter and added his credit card to the pile. A man flipped the papers over and studied them. McGriffin turned and leaned against the counter. "Depends on the pilot, too. If he's good, he can miss the roughest spots."

Vikki cocked an amused eyebrow at him. "And you're good?"

"The best." McGriffin grinned. The attendant pushed a key and a logbook across the counter. McGriffin grabbed them and opened the door for Vikki.

Heat rose in shimmering waves across the asphalt apron. The planes were secured to the ground by a series of ropes. They sat thirty to fifty feet apart from each other, lined up and pointing toward the taxiway. McGriffin pulled out the logbook and glanced at the numbers embossed on the front. Looking around, he spotted a small Cessna with a matching number.

Reaching the craft, he walked quickly around, inspecting the engine, flaps, fuselage, and tail. Vikki followed him, fascinated with the thoroughness with which he scrutinized the small craft. She followed him as he ducked under the tail section.

"That seems a lot of work."

McGriffin put his hand up against the vertical stabilizer. "What?"

"You know, pilots are supposed to be all macho and that. Man against the wild, jumping into the open cockpit and going one on one against nature. You look like you don't trust whoever got the plane ready for you."

McGriffin wiggled the stabilizer, then stepped back. He wiped grease from his hands. "I don't. I figure it's my life at stake, so I need to take time to make sure the thing works the way it's supposed to." He unfastened a securing line and quickly gathered it in.

Vikki put a hand up to her face, shielding her eyes from the glare. "They do it in the movies."

"When machines get this sophisticated, something's bound to go wrong. You just can't 'kick the tires and light the fires' anymore. Come on." He boosted her up into the plane and showed her how to buckle the shoulder straps.

McGriffin started the engine and eased the Cessna out from the parking apron. His eyes flew over the gauges: attitude, oil pressure, temperature, rpm—the Cessna had ten times fewer instruments than he was used to in a C-141, but the danger of flying remained the same. If he used any less concentration, it could be the last time he'd ever fly.

Vikki spoke to him, interrupting his train of thought.

"Sorry." McGriffin shook his head and grinned at

her. "I get so wrapped up in this, I tune everything out. What did you say?"

"Where are we going?"

"Besides up? Nowhere in particular. I thought we'd just try to catch some of the sights. Is there anywhere you'd like to go?"

"Well, I was up in the mountains a few weeks ago. How about there?"

"No problem." Turning the small craft, he scanned the sky for incoming traffic. The tower gave him permission to proceed onto the runway. He pulled off the taxiway and onto the immense strip of asphalt. The end of the runway disappeared two miles away, engulfed in a shimmering mirage of water.

"Ready?" Not waiting for an answer, he brought the engine to full throttle and started down the runway.

McGriffin kept his eyes on the runway, periodically flicking them to the instrument panel. They passed a huge marker on the side displaying the number 13. In the distance, spaced every thousand feet, the numbers 12, 11, and on down to 1 were visible. He glanced at Vikki. "Put your hands on the wheel. When I say 'now,' pull gently back on it."

As the airspeed indicator rose, McGriffin waited, until, "All right—now."

Vikki jerked her wheel. McGriffin stopped the wheels from coming all the way back and instead eased them to a set position.

The small craft left the runway with plenty of length to spare. McGriffin said, "Congratulations. You've just taken off for the first time. Try flying us up to altitude." He kept a hand loosely on his wheel.

Vikki kept her eyes straight ahead, seriously trying to keep the plane in a constant ascent. "The runway's so long. Why did they build it like that if we didn't need all of it?"

"The aero club uses Wendover Air Force Base's runway—it's over two miles long for the military aircraft." McGriffin didn't finish saying that it was that long only because of the nuclear weapons at Alpha Base. The old weapons were so large and unwieldy that they needed an extra-large runway to ensure that the transports had plenty of room to take off with the additional weight.

McGriffin banked the aircraft in a gentle turn, heading toward the mountains. Vikki mimicked his movements. McGriffin said, "Say, you're pretty good at this. Are you sure you haven't flown before?"

"This is my first time in a cockpit."

"I'll have to work on my instructor's license so I can get you a pilot's license for yourself."

She laughed. "I said I liked it—not do it every day."

McGriffin took them out of the bank. "All right, I've got the aircraft. Just show me the way."

Vikki looked down at the ground. "I can't tell where we are."

McGriffin pointed out a double strip of roads below them. "That's the interstate. Wendover Air Force Base is below us, and Nevada is to the left."

"Uh, follow I-80 west. It's about five exits before you turn north."

The sand gave way to the barren mountains. They encountered some chop, but it was still early enough to miss the afternoon turbulence. McGriffin flew in a broken path, avoiding flying over dark patches on the ground. The dark patches heated up faster than the surrounding lighter area, causing air turbulence. "We're over the mountains. Anywhere in particular you want to go?"

Vikki studied the area below her. Every so often a dirt road sliced through the valleys. For the most part the mountains were untouched by human presence.

"Follow that road. It should take us to where I was last week. It's kind of hard telling where I am, though."

"It takes time." McGriffin brought the aircraft down in altitude, finally leveling off at a thousand feet above ground level. "How's this?"

"Better." She continued to stare out the cockpit.

The mountains grew rougher the farther north they flew. McGriffin managed to keep a good blend between following the dirt road and keeping away from the thermals. Trees started appearing on the mountains. The plane bumped, hitting areas of turbulence he could not circumvent.

Vikki motioned excitedly. "There. The meadow in that ring of peaks. I remember it from a map I was looking at." The mountain looked sheared off, resembling a crater from an ancient volcano. A pointed ridge encircled the meadow. Set down into the crater's walls, the meadow looked nearly a mile long. A pond sat at the low end of the meadow; the other end lay against a sharp rise of peaks.

McGriffin banked the Cessna, bringing it to within a few hundred feet of the crest. "I could almost land in there."

"Would it be hard?"

McGriffin studied the crater. "No. There's plenty of room."

"You're not going to try it, are you?"

"And chance getting stuck? No thanks. I've got to work tonight." He pulled up and buzzed the ridge. "How did you find this place?"

"I just wanted to get away, do some camping. It's nice down there."

McGriffin was silent. He pulled up and brought the aircraft around. "I know what you mean." He glanced at his watch. "We're approaching the one-hour mark. I've got to get back."

"You're worse than Cinderella. Can't you go to work a little late?"

"And turn into a pumpkin? Maybe some other day. I've got some errands to run before getting to work."

They followed the same dirt road back, keeping at a higher altitude to avoid the thermals. They kept to themselves most of the way. McGriffin broke the silence.

"What brings you out here, Vikki?"

"A job."

"What do you do?"

She turned and looked out the window. "I'd rather not talk about it."

"Okay." McGriffin drew in a breath. It always seemed the women he got introduced to either treated him like a brother or a jerk—which gave credence to being unequally yoked. And that brought his thoughts back to Linda. He flew without speaking.

Vikki turned from the window. "Bill, I like you a lot, but for a while let's just keep out of each other's past. I've got some things to sort out."

McGriffin mulled it over. "Sounds fair. I guess I'm in the same boat." He shrugged. His hopes flickered, and he felt strangely content. Vikki was really different. She wasn't as glamorous as Linda, but she was more self-assured. That's it—it was a sense of self-confidence Vikki possessed, a worldliness—yet not egotistical. He thought briefly about asking her about her beliefs, but got cold feet—he had been burned too many times to be laughed at.

McGriffin dismissed the thought and felt angry with himself. Glancing over at her, she smiled at him and turned back to looking out the window.

Here he'd gone out with her only once, and he was already thinking like a teenager. They flew back in silence, warm in each other's presence.

11

Picnic Area outside of Alpha Base

Britnell pulled a jug of wine from the picnic basket. He threw a smile at Vikki as he screwed open the top. High class, mused Vikki. Twist-top wine.

A helicopter beat overhead, flying away from Alpha Base. Vikki concentrated on the inside of the fence while Britnell poured the wine. The barracks, security building, and command post were arranged in a tight knot just inside the four fences. The picnic area seemed like an oasis in the shadow of the fortresslike Alpha Base. She compared the view with the drawings on the map Britnell had slipped her. The words FOR OFFICIAL USE ONLY were scratched out on the top and bottom of the document.

Britnell shoved Vikki a glass of pink Chablis. It tasted like wet cardboard, but she sipped delicately on it. She leaned back and ran a hand across his arm.

95

"I wish you didn't have to go on duty. Seven days is a long time not to see you."

Britnell broke into a smile. "There's a way I might be able to get around that."

"Really?"

"I was saving it for a surprise. I checked with my first sergeant. He's scheduled my partner, Clayborn, and me on the Omega shift this week, patrolling Alpha Base from outside the fence. That killer rabbit we tracked down three weeks ago impressed the hell out of him, so he's giving us a break."

"Outside shift?"

"Yeah. One of the crews gets to patrol the area outside of Alpha Base instead of pulling guard duty inside."

"Ummm. So we *can* see each other." She leaned over and kissed him lightly on the cheek. "Why don't I give you a call when I'm free?"

"Sure. When?"

Vikki thought rapidly—Harding needed at least a twenty-four-hour heads-up before starting the raid, and she still needed to get the call signs. "Let's plan on tomorrow night, nine-thirty, unless I call."

Britnell threw back the glass and chugged the wine. He poured himself another glass. "You got it. Tomorrow night, nine-thirty, unless I hear otherwise. We'll meet right here, and I'll take you out with us."

She leaned over. She pushed him back onto the ground and kissed him hard. "What I've got in mind, I think maybe just you should show up and leave your partner back home."

Britnell thought it over as Vikki kissed his neck; he caressed her hair and grinned. "Yeah. Clayborn can take a siesta. No problem."

Vikki held him tight for some minutes. Rolling

over, she brought up the map that he had given her. She studied the paper and waited a minute until he downed another glass. "What are these symbols?"

Britnell grabbed for the area map of Alpha Base and stabbed at the markings designated P, T, S, and M. "These are pressure, temperature, sonic, and motion sensors. Your company will have to avoid them when they build the new barracks. They're buried all over the place."

She folded the map and leaned over to kiss his neck. "I can't wait until I see you again."

"I'd like to see you tonight, but the first evening of my shift overlaps with the last shift's—it's all briefings for us tonight. But at least I'll be there with a buzz on." He eyed the remaining bottle of wine. "Want any more?" Vikki shook her head. He grinned lopsidedly and polished it off.

1310 local

Wendover, Utah

Vikki checked the number in the Wendover AFB phone book one more time before she dialed. Three phone numbers were listed under Base Operations. She dialed the first, and as the phone rang, she hoped she had picked the right number.

"Base Ops."

Vikki spoke quickly and tried to sound frantic. "My boyfriend is flying into Wendover tomorrow night. Is there any way to find out when he's scheduled to arrive?"

A bored voice answered, "Do you have a call sign?"

"No, I don't." Vikki bit her lip. She knew that all

aircraft used call signs, or a code name, to identify themselves over the radio; with the proper call sign, it was easy to masquerade as another plane. But according to Harding, the Air Force changed their call signs periodically.

"We usually don't have the flights posted until several hours before they get here . . . but I have a C-130 out of Peterson AFB, Colorado, scheduled to get in at 2300 hours. Does that help?"

"Yes, it does. Do you have its call sign?"

"Merry Zero Three."

"Thank you." After she hung up, she dialed again, carefully punching in the international access code for Baja. The phone was answered on the seventh ring.

"Harding."

"Tomorrow night at eleven o'clock a C-130 is due to land at Wendover. I've got the call sign."

"Good. We can fly into Wendover AFB using that call sign a half hour before it's due and not raise any suspicion; but it gives us only a half hour to get everything unloaded. What about the IFF? Are you going to be able to get hold of one to get around Alpha Base's sensors?"

Remembering Britnell's boast of having an IFF on his Bronco, Vikki said, "I should be able to do it."

It sounded like Harding placed a hand over the receiver; he came back a minute later. "Okay, tomorrow night is the night. We'll meet you at the staging area tomorrow morning, sunrise." The line went dead.

Vikki hung up, flush with excitement that the assault was coming together.

1640 local

Wendover, Nevada

"A penny for your thoughts."

"Huh?" Vikki shook her head. McGriffin sat across from her and dabbed at his mouth with a napkin. Vikki flushed, suddenly feeling foolish that she hadn't been listening to him. "Sorry. I was just thinking."

"I could tell." McGriffin pushed his vegetables to one side of his plate. He cut into his prime rib, took a bit. "I really appreciate you spending an early dinner with me."

"What?" Vikki swung her hand around, taking in the casino. "And miss all this?"

McGriffin laughed. "I know four in the afternoon isn't good for the appetite, but since I have to work—"

Vikki placed a hand on top of McGriffin's. He stopped talking. She smiled. "I said, don't worry about it. It's nice to be able to just talk. Besides, like I said, I'll be gone for a few weeks."

"I'm glad you told me. Maybe we can see each other when you get back."

"Yeah." She set her mouth.

He didn't move his hand. She felt awkward at first, like a teenager. But it felt so *good* just to be able to sit and talk, and know he wasn't trying to get her in bed. Withdrawing her hand, she toyed with her food. "So don't you ever get a break?"

"We're kind of shorthanded now—but I thought we weren't going to pry into each other's life."

"You're right." She took a bite and chewed slowly,

99

watching him. McGriffin cut at his steak and wolfed the food down; but unlike Britnell—or Harding, for that matter—even in his haste his manners were impeccable.

She toyed with her food. "You know, when we first met, you said you didn't go out and do the tourist bit. Especially where you used to live."

McGriffin swallowed. "Yeah. I could never seem to find the time to relax, enjoy the sights. I've always had to have something going on. You know, busy jogging, working on the house . . ." He drew quiet at the mention of his house, as if something bothered him.

Vikki studied his face. His dark hair was stylishly cut, but it was a bit on the short side, even though it was long compared to how Britnell wore his hair. McGriffin was solidly built and quite good-looking; and even though he was suddenly withdrawn, he had a playful gleam in his eye. Whatever had been in his past, she would be very surprised if he had not been intimately involved with someone. She felt close to him.

Vikki said, "I know what you mean. I grew up in Colorado and never got a chance to see some of the touristy areas, like Pikes Peak, Garden of the Gods, the Air Force Academy—" McGriffin started coughing. Vikki frowned. "Are you all right?"

"Fine. I'm okay." McGriffin wiped at his mouth. He wet his lips as if he wanted to say something.

Vikki cocked her head. "Is anything the matter?"

"No." He picked up his fork. "Ah, where in Colorado did you say you lived?"

"Monument. That's about ten miles from Colorado Springs, just north of the Air Force Academy."

McGriffin's eyes widened. "Yeah, I know."

"You do? How's that?"

He cut a slice of prime rib. "It's a long story." He

glanced at his watch. "Uh, I've really got to hurry. Do you think we can get together for a real date after you get back—you know, spend some time where I don't have to worry about getting to work?"

"Sure." Vikki smiled and brushed back her hair. She didn't know when she could make it, but even if she had to come back to Wendover as a fugitive, McGriffin would be worth the risk. He seeme to be everything that Harding had never turned out to be.

What's more, McGriffin was just the thing she needed to get her mind off the assault.

12

Saturday, 18 June, 0547 local

*Humboldt National Forest
One Hundred Miles Northwest of Wendover*

Standing in the Chevy van's door, Vikki pushed her hair from her eyes. The sun just peeked over the eastern range, bringing a flood of warming sunlight. It wasn't cold enough to see her breath, but she shivered just the same. The additional five thousand feet in altitude from Wendover was more than enough to cause the chill.

The air smelled of ozone—the pine-fresh vigor of mountain living. The wind whooshed through the trees, sounding spooky. She'd almost be willing to give up everything to stay there forever.

And bury her head in the sand, ignoring the atrocities that lay waiting at Alpha Base.

No, she was too involved to back down now. She

glanced at her watch and waited for the sound that would start it all.

Another ten minutes passed before she heard it. The plane's engines bounced off the mountainsides, rolling down the meadow. The roar grew in intensity; it violated the serenity hanging in the valley. Purple and yellow flowers waved in the fields, seeming to beckon the plane on.

Suddenly, the plane popped over the crest line. It dove for the meadow, making an impossible turn, flying past trees and house-size boulders. Engines roaring, the black C-130 seemed to fall from the sky. Cliffs guarded one end of the meadow. A gentle slope led to a lake, ringed with trees, at the opposite end. The four-engine craft dropped for the pond.

Its wheels barely clipped the treetops. The plane hit the edge of the meadow and bounced twice. Its engines shook the ground as they reversed, slowing the low-slung craft. Dust and decapitated flowers sprayed up into the air, covering the airplane in a fog of debris.

Vikki squinted and placed a hand over her eyes. The C-130 transport emerged from the dust. It traveled the mile stretch, reaching the end of the meadow, and turning just before reaching the cliffs.

When Harding told her of the mercenary's C-130, Vikki consulted *Jane's All the World's Aircraft* to find out for herself about the squat four-engined transport. An ultrareliable troop carrier, the model L-100-30 C-130 Hercules "stretch Herky bird" played many roles. It carried troops, airlifted supplies, dropped twenty-thousand-pound bombs, inserted airborne rangers, recovered satellites, scooped up pails of water from the ocean—the list was almost endless. Obtained from a second party, the elongated civilian version of the military C-130 was as much of a legend as the old "Gooney Bird."

Vikki's eyebrows rose; she was impressed. She had had her doubts about using the remote mountain meadow as a staging area, but any second thoughts were dashed by seeing the transport's performance. She lowered her hands, pulled her jacket closer to her, and stepped down from the van.

A door opened from the C-130's side. A tall, erect man dressed in khaki jumped nimbly from the craft as it slowed to a halt. Anthony Harding followed. He stumbled slightly. The tall man steadied him and they both jogged to Vikki. The engines slowed, falling in pitch.

The man flashed Vikki a smile. He slapped his hands together to keep them warm as they approached. "Ms. Osborrn?" She nodded. "I'm Colonel Macklin Renault. Is everything ready?"

Vikki nodded, her mouth tight.

"The moving van?"

"It's outside my apartment."

Harding reached into the back and pulled a jacket from the van. He asked, "What about the call signs?"

Vikki reached into the front and dug a sheet of paper from the glove compartment. She handed it over to Renault. "These are valid until tomorrow night. As I told Anthony, Wendover is expecting a C-130 from Peterson Air Force Base in Colorado to land and refuel at eleven o'clock tonight. You have to be on time to get there before him."

Renault studied the sheet, then folded it and placed it in his top pocket. "Good. We'll have half an hour before anyone discovers there are two C-130's. By that time my C-130 will be gone and the attack will be under way."

Harding blew on his hands, trying to warm them in the morning cold. "Might as well have your men get out and relax, Colonel. They're not going anywhere for a while."

Renault paid Harding sparse attention. He scanned the mountains that formed a near-perfect bowl around them. "Have you seen anybody up here?"

"No."

"I still don't like this. We're too much in the open." He turned and studied the trees. "There's not enough foliage to cover the plane. We'll have to pull out the camouflage." He started for the C-130.

Harding ignored him and climbed into the van. Vikki frowned, and ran after Renault. "What's going on?" She caught up with him. Renault took long strides, not slowing down for Vikki.

"The aircraft stands out like a sore thumb. If anyone sees it, it will blow our cover."

"I told you we're alone."

"If you made it here, Ms. Osborrn, then anyone else could, too. But it's not the hikers or campers I'm worried about. It's what's up in the air. We flew in low enough to avoid radar, but now that we're on the ground, the whole area is probably under a random satellite surveillance, designed to spot any infiltration such as this."

"But the plane is in the shadows."

"That doesn't stop it from emitting in the infrared. We've got to get some cover on it." They reached the combat door. Renault swung aboard and Vikki followed seconds later.

As her eyes adjusted to the darkness, she counted fifty men lining the front side of the transport. They sat on webbed pallet seating, watching her in silence. A vehicle took up half the back of the stretched C-130. APC—Armored Personnel Carrier, she thought. She had done her homework well. She'd made sure she knew everything about their weapons.

Constructed of a composite hull, the APC was originally designed for use by the Marines. Ceramic tiles were sandwiched in between an outer aluminum skin and an inner skin of reinforced fiberglass. When an armor-piercing shell tried to penetrate the APC's body, the tiles would shatter, diffusing the shell's energy through its body.

Renault ran a hand proudly across the APC's body; his demeanor seemed to suddenly change. "You can thank your military-industrial complex for this, Ms. Osborrn. One or two simple bribes, and its delivery to a third party was never accomplished. I wonder how many more we could have ordered before we were caught."

Vikki answered coolly, "If you're so against our military-industrial complex, Colonel, then why aren't you doing this for free?"

Renault scowled. Turning, he snapped an order. A crew of five men scurried to the rear, squeezing past the APC. A jump door opened in the back, allowing light to peek into the darkened aircraft. The men pushed out a bag.

Stepping outside, Vikki backed away from the C-130. The crew pulled a camouflaged mesh from the bag. Renault bellowed at the troops in the plane. Men poured out to help cover the C-130 with the meshlike material.

Ten of the men rolled a hose and pump down to the lake. After the mesh was in place, two men took turns pumping water by cranking on a long lever. As pressure built up, Renault directed the water onto the C-130's engines. It was twenty minutes before the men retired to the trees. Even though the morning air was still chilly, they peeled off their shirts, sweating from the exertion.

From the van the C-130 resembled a lump of dark

wet cloth. Renault explained how the water had cooled the plane enough to prevent infrared hot spots. "If they study their satellite photos close enough, they'll find us, but the mesh will hide us from a casual look. The water should have cooled it down enough not to warrant that additional high-resolution photograph."

Renault went over the plan with Harding and Vikki, hammering out details. When everyone was satisfied, Renault suggested that they try and catch up on some sleep. The night was going to be a long one.

Harding and Vikki climbed in the back of the Chevy van. Renault's men spread out to nap under the trees. Within minutes the meadow was deserted. Vikki and Harding could have been alone in the mountains if they didn't know better. Inside the van Harding fumbled around the wheel well. He cursed moments later.

"Where's the dope?"

Vikki wordlessly reached for the grass she had hidden.

Harding quickly rolled a joint, licked the length of it, and lit up. After several hits he leaned back and offered it to her. She shook her head. Harding drew in another breath of marijuana. He studied Vikki before asking, "What's wrong?"

Silence. Vikki looked away, then said, "Nothing."

Harding allowed her to sit quietly as he toked. "I haven't seen you this quiet for years."

Vikki shrugged. "Just thinking." About McGriffin? she thought. No, that wasn't it—even though McGriffin would have never have been so . . . grating. She brushed back her hair. "After all this time, talking, planning . . . I just hope we can pull it off."

"You covered your part, didn't you?"

"Yeah."

107

"And if Britnell is as stupid as you say, we've got it made." He held out the marijuana to her. Again she shook her head.

Harding frowned and let the smoke curl up from his mouth. "You aren't falling for that kid, are you?"

Vikki's eyes flashed. "I *told* you—"

"Okay, that's enough." Harding leaned back. He shook his head. "I don't know. You've been acting strange lately—preoccupied."

"We're only taking on the largest nuclear weapons repository in the free world, and you expect me *not* to be preoccupied?" Vikki curled up in one corner of the van, shutting her eyes and using one of the duffel bags thrown in the rear as a pillow. A moment passed. Harding stirred, then she felt a hand on her shoulder. He kissed her cheek.

"It's been a long time . . ." His hand moved down and cupped her breast.

She didn't move. Harding kissed her again. When she didn't respond, he moved away from her. Vikki waited, tense. Moments later his breathing deepened. She felt the tension drain from her, then started trembling.

The pressures from the past few weeks seemed to cascade around her. Britnell, Anthony, she thought. It seemed like they'd forgotten she could do anything but have sex. McGriffin had been the only one she could relax with, the only one who hadn't threatened her.

And she didn't even know him.

As she fell asleep, she felt she didn't even know herself.

13

Saturday, 18 June, 1800 local

Wendover, Nevada

"Hurry up. Climb inside." Vikki pulled the moving van that she had rented up to her apartment. Harding waved the group into the back of the van. Ten of Renault's men, dressed in black jump suits, climbed inside. Each carried a rifle wrapped in blankets. One flicked a cigarette out before pulling himself up. Hours before, they had driven to Vikki's apartment in the Chevy van, leaving Renault and the rest of the men up in the mountains.

The men tried to find a place to make themselves comfortable as Harding began to close the door. "All right. Remember—no matter what happens, *no one* says anything. As soon as I lock you in, no talking until we open you up. Any questions?"

Harding was met by silence. Vikki and Harding struggled with two twin mattresses, positioning them upright at the rear of the moving van, blocking both entrance and exit. Satisfied that the mattresses would provide a credible cover if the back were inadvertently opened, they shut the door and locked it.

Harding wiped his hands on his jeans. "Ready?"

Vikki flipped him the keys. "If you have any trouble, leave the talking to me—the guards know me. And be careful starting out. First gear is tricky."

Harding replied by stepping up into the moving van. Vikki climbed into the smaller Chevy van. She waited until Harding familiarized himself with the rented moving van before pulling away from the apartment. She shielded her eyes from the sun; it would set in another hour.

The truck rumbled behind her. The gears crunched as Harding tried switching too fast.

Vikki adjusted the rearview mirror. That's all we need, she thought. Calling off the assault because klutzo can't drive a stick shift.

As they left Wendover, the boulevard to the base narrowed to a two-lane road. She purposely went slow, allowing cars to pass them. The usual twenty-minute trip expanded to forty minutes, giving her time to go over the plan in her head.

She had tried to think of everything, but there were too many ifs left unanswered: *if* Britnell didn't mess up meeting her; *if* Renault made the rendezvous on time; *if* the helicopters showed up; *if* Wendover AFB communications were totally cut; *if* they could take out the barracks.

A sign announcing Wendover AFB jolted her thoughts. Constructed of brick and glass, the guard shack that defended Wendover AFB's main gate had two lanes of pavement running on either side of it. Vikki slowed and flashed her visitor's pass. A young security policeman stepped from the shack.

Vikki's heart froze. She didn't recognize the airman. The guard waved the car in front of her on, then held up a hand when he failed to spot a base decal on Vikki's van. Vikki unrolled her window and held out the pass. "How's it going?"

The airman's eyes widened at her smile. "Fine." He barely looked at the pass and instead looked into her eyes. "Can I help you?"

Vikki pointed to the yellow pass on the windshield. "Is there a problem?"

The young man flushed. "No, ma'am. Just didn't see the pass. Go ahead."

Vikki started to roll away. "Thanks. And see you around."

"Sure. No problem." He straightened his ascot and waved her van on past. She was inside the base when he turned to the moving van behind her. Vikki pulled off the side of the road, just past the guard shack, and waited for Harding. The young airman read a sheaf of papers that Harding had thrust at him. After shuffling through the papers, the airman shook his head and pointed back outside the gate.

"Shit." Vikki's breath quickened. The airman and Harding started arguing. She flung open the door. Brushing back her hair, she stepped toward the guard shack. Harding was giving the airman his best rap.

"I tell you, man, I'm supposed to deliver this shipment to the airman's barracks. Open your eyes and read: 'Airman First Class Britnell, 1977th Security Police Squadron, Wendover Air Force Base: partial shipment.' It can't get any clearer than that."

"This does not have the transportation officer's stamp on it, sir. I'm sorry, but I can't allow you on base."

Vikki stepped up to the guard. "What seems to be the problem?"

"I'm sorry, ma'am, but—" he stopped as he turned to her. His voice softened. "Excuse me, miss. What do you have to do with this?"

"Airman Britnell is my boyfriend. This partial shipment is some new furniture he stashed at my place before I moved out here." She clamped her mouth, hoping she wouldn't get tripped up in a lie. She looked around. "Come on, ask your partner. He knows me." She hoped that his partner wasn't a new security guard as well.

The airman shook his head. "I'm sorry, miss. I can't allow this truck on base." A car honked, impatiently waiting to be saluted onto Wendover. "Excuse me." The security policemen waved a half-dozen cars past.

"There must be something you can do." Another car honked.

He spoke over his shoulder. "Sorry—"

"What's going on, Saunders?" A tech sergeant stepped from the shack, wiping his hands of a sandwich he placed down.

The young airman turned, still waving cars into the base. "This van wants to get on base, Sergeant. The papers don't—"

"Well, hello, Vikki," interrupted the sergeant. He broke into a smile. "Are you causing this traffic tie-up?"

Vikki brushed back her hair. Her heart slowed. "Oh, Fred. Am I glad you're here." She motioned toward the moving van. "A partial shipment arrived for Britnell—I'm trying to help out. It's some furniture he bought and I wanted to surprise him."

The sergeant shook his head. "No problem. With the way that boy's straightened up, I'd let you bring a fleet of trucks on base. You've been good for him." He waved Harding on through. "Get going. You're holding up traffic."

"Thanks, Fred."

"Take care, Vikki." The sergeant turned to the young airman. "Carry on, Saunders. This isn't a Air Training Command base—use a little judgment next time." He stomped into the guard shack to his sandwich.

Harding pulled behind Vikki's van and waited for her to move out. Once the van was on the road, Vikki's leg started shaking. She drew in a deep breath. "Settle down," she said to herself, "This is just the beginning."

She followed the road to a tee. A sign at the intersection pointed to the right and listed: BASE HEADQUARTERS, CBPO/CPO, OFFICERS' CLUB, BX, COMMISSARY, RV PARKING. The sign pointing left listed both the airmen's barracks and Alpha Base. Vikki wet her lips and made a sudden decision. Turning right, she headed for the RV parking. Harding hesitated at the intersection, then followed her.

The lot was half filled with Winnebagos, land cruisers, thirty-foot trailers, and an assortment of campers. The gate was open. Vikki pulled in and found a spot between two Winnebagos.

Harding maneuvered the moving van, squeezing into an open slot. Vikki hopped from the Chevy van. He met her, his face gray. "What the hell are you doing? We're supposed to park by the barracks and use Britnell as our cover story."

"And probably get caught by that airman at the gate," she retorted. "He wasn't too thrilled about being countermanded in front of us. What do you think he'll do when he gets back to the barracks tonight and finds the moving van still there?"

"We could leave a note that we were waiting for Britnell."

Vikki threw up her hands. "And when they find out

he's still got six days to go before he can leave Alpha Base, we'll be up shit's creek. Think, Anthony. It would have worked if we hadn't brought attention to ourselves. We've got to throw that plan out the window and start over." She kicked at the pavement. "No one will think of looking for us here. So we just lay low until we rendezvous with Renault."

Harding mulled it over. The color returned to his cheeks. "All right. I guess it doesn't matter where we park, as long as we don't get caught." He looked around, and seeing no movement, said, "Let's climb in your van. Time to wait it out. We've got two hours."

"Yeah." Vikki turned for the Chevy van as Harding opened up the back of the moving van, allowing air to enter, yet keeping the mattress in place so the men would be hidden from view.

Might as well be in the friggin' military, she thought. Hurry up and wait.

Wendover AFB Command Post

The guard nodded McGriffin past. "Evening, Major."

McGriffin broke off his whistle. "Good evening, Farquer. How are you tonight?"

"Fine, sir, and yourself?"

"Couldn't be better. Well, yes it could. I could be going off duty instead of going on." His thoughts turned to Vikki, and he felt a warm, peaceful sensation. He'd really have to open up with her next time they met, try and overcome this phobia he had about telling her he was in the military.

"I know what you mean, sir."

"Have a good one."

"You too, sir." Airman Farquer palmed open the door to the command post.

Any tension in the chamber vanished when McGriffin walked in. McGriffin sensed a lifting of spirits, a change in atmosphere from the day shift, when the other two officers-of-the-day reigned.

Chief Zolley stood at his elbow. As usual, McGriffin didn't hear the chief master sergeant arrive as Zolley appeared at his side.

"Good evening, Major. Ready for your briefing?"

"Let's have it." McGriffin slipped into his chair overlooking the dimly lit room. He swiveled around and eyed the status board. A series of green lights burned steadily on each display. The MILLER clock still pointed to 1700. "Anything up, Chief?"

Zolley handed him a packet marked SECRET. "Nothing much, sir. All communication links are up. AUTODIN verifies our status, and we've got six more days until a shift change at Alpha Base. The only incoming aircraft scheduled are some T-38's on a cross-country and a C-130 out of Peterson Field." He shuffled a page. "The 130's call sign is Merry Zero Three with an ETA of 2300 local."

"There's a reserve unit there." McGriffin tapped his desk. "I've got a classmate stationed at Pete—Moose Monahan. Remind me when they get in, Chief. I want to check them out, see if Moose might be on board."

"They're not remaining overnight, sir. They've got wheels up scheduled at 2320."

"That's strange." McGriffin frowned. "You'd think they'd R.O.N. being so far from home. Those reserve weanies just don't appreciate remote garden spots." He cocked his hands behind his head. "What's going on outside the base?"

"I've included a few messages in the briefing packet that was twixted this afternoon—nothing critical."

McGriffin flipped through the packet. "All nice and quiet." He handed the classified bundle back to

Zolley. "Thanks, Chief. It looks like another slow one. That's all I've got."

"Thanks, sir." Chief Zolley disappeared as quickly as he had materialized. McGriffin leaned back and watched the board for a few minutes. Another quiet evening. That's all right, he thought. I've got plenty to keep me busy.

Once he had gotten used to the routine, McGriffin took advantage of the spare time. It was too early to nap. He trusted the crew, and with his amicable attitude, the best people pushed to get on his shift. It didn't matter that it was the night shift—working under McGriffin was a "good deal." Or so Zolley had clued him in.

It would be even better if he had someone to talk to, a peer to shoot the bull with. He never saw the other two officers from the command post—he assumed they just weren't sociable. Manny Yarnez was all right, but Manny's schedule was nearly as erratic as his. The rest of the chopper pilots all worked during the day, so it was difficult to find a friend. And other than Lieutenant Felowmate on Alpha Base, he shied away from the security policemen. They were a different breed altogether—more like Marines than Air Force.

But now that he'd met Vikki, at least he didn't starve for conversation anymore.

He reached in his drawer and pulled out a programmed text from Air Command and Staff College: *Stability and Structure of Third World Forces.* He sighed. As much as he hated it, this was the perfect time to do his "professional military education."

Oh, well. It might be too early to nap now, but once he started reading, it would knock him out better than any sleeping pill.

14

Wendover AFB, Utah

Vikki glanced at her watch for the fifth time in ten minutes. She put up her hair, keeping it from getting in the way. She then slipped off the tank top and quickly stretched her arms through the brassiere. Clasping the snap, she pulled on a dark, long-sleeve top. The bra was snug—it had been a while since she'd even considered wearing one—but there was too much at stake tonight to be caught swinging free. She just hoped it wouldn't cramp her movements.

A quick glimpse at her watch caused her to move to the front of the van. Harding sat quietly smoking, the cigarette smoke immersing him in a dim purple haze. A single light shone from high above them, starkly illuminating the RV parking lot. Harding didn't turn as he spoke.

"Is everything ready?"

"If Britnell doesn't screw up, I'll be at the end of the runway by a quarter after ten."

"That doesn't leave you much time."

"It's enough."

This is it . . . everything we've been waiting for. She felt she should be excited, dizzy with what they were about to do. *Then why do I feel like crap?*

Harding took a drag from his cigarette. "Good luck." He opened the passenger door and slipped out, cupping the cigarette so it couldn't be seen.

Vikki wiggled to the front. She checked the mirrors, door locks, and finally the gas gauge before rubbing her hands across the wheel. She drew in a breath.

She pulled slowly past the moving van, and thought she could make out a shadow in the front seat. Squinting, she couldn't see him. Wherever Harding had hidden, he made himself scarce.

The fence around the RV storage lot was locked. Base personnel must have bolted the gate. A chain cutter quickly put that obstacle aside. Once outside the gate, she secured the fence so it looked locked.

The road to the main part of Wendover AFB was deserted. Light spilled from the officers' club, full of the Saturday night crowd. The chance of running into someone was slim—and so far she still headed toward the airmen's barracks. Her excuse of visiting Britnell would hold up if she were stopped.

She left the barracks and enlisted club behind her after the next stop sign. She glanced at her watch. Five after nine. An hour and a half. She sped up slightly as she rounded the end of the runway. Alpha Base was still five miles away.

The van raced down a hill, then up the other side. As she rounded the top, the Pit opened up in front of her. Individual lights demarcating storage bunkers shone with a ghostly yellow tinge. High-pressure 400-

watt sodium lights splashed their glare around the four fences surrounding Alpha Base. The main entrance looked like a stage setting for a Hollywood movie: strobes and red and yellow flickering lights flashed crazily off the metal mesh enveloping the front gate. Gargantuan vehicles moved inside the complex, slow, dark, and of uncertain shape.

Vikki stared, mesmerized by the site. Alpha Base took on an entirely different character at night. Instead of the laid-back desert storage facility, it resembled a waiting behemoth, growling, eyes flashing, waiting to devour anything that dared pass its way.

She looked down. Her foot held the accelerator to the floor—she was traveling close to eighty. She let up on the pedal, slowing to the speed limit. The motion calmed her, forcing her thoughts away from Alpha Base. It was one thing to meet Britnell on time. It was another thing to be stopped speeding. She might not be so lucky knowing one of the security policemen this time.

She slowed further as she approached Alpha Base's main entrance. A guard started to step out of the guard shack when she turned left for the picnic area. He watched her as she drove past.

If Britnell's information was correct, security had tracked her once she was within five miles of Alpha Base. That corresponded to when she rounded the end of the runway. As long as she did nothing threatening, she'd be left alone. She wondered how conspicuous the van would be at the picnic area.

Ten vehicles were parked along the field with their lights turned out. Vikki drove the van to the opposite side of the field, turned off the ignition, and relaxed. Radios played softly. Once in a while the red taillights of a car would blink. Giggling came from the general area. Kids parking, she thought. That makes it even better. Who'd think of questioning a van parked at one of Wendover's necking spots? She fit right in with the military brats living on base with their parents.

The minutes passed. *Nine twenty-five.* Renault was landing in an hour. It was at least ten minutes to the deserted hangar at the end of the runway where she was to rendezvous with Harding and the C-130. Everything was going to go whether she showed up or not.

After another five minutes she started the engine. She had to warn Harding—if Britnell didn't show, they wouldn't have the IFF and were as good as dead. She jerked the van into gear and started off. Approaching the entrance, she slammed on her brakes to avoid hitting a car—

A military four-wheel-drive—a Ford Bronco— pulled into the parking lot. *Britnell!*

The Bronco pulled up beside her. Britnell emerged. He looked carefully around. They were far enough away from the kids so as not to bring attention to themselves.

As he approached the van, she got another attack of the "ifs." Everything was fine: *if* Britnell was alone; *if* she could make it back undetected—the "ifs" piled up even as he reached for the door.

"Hi, babe. I ditched Clayborn for a couple of hours."

Vikki didn't answer. She leaned into him with a long kiss. "I want to do something exciting tonight." Vikki held his head in her hands. She kissed him hard. "Your Bronco—in the desert. Now."

"You're on." Britnell jumped from the van and strode to the Bronco.

As they climbed in, Vikki leaned over and ran a hand over his chest. "Hurry."

Britnell jerked the Bronco into gear. A wide grin

covered his face. "It's only been a day since I've seen you, babe."

"It seems like a year."

Britnell turned toward the main entrance. "Anywhere in particular?"

"Somewhere back off the main road. I want to get off while looking at Alpha Base."

"You got it."

Vikki smiled in the dark and leaned back in her seat. She stole a glance at her watch. *Nine thirty-six—plenty of time.*

Britnell turned onto the main road. They bounced as he floored the accelerator. The road whipped by. He looked over and caught her smiling. He patted her thigh. "Man, am I glad to see you. We've been going crazy doing one exercise after another. You'd think they'd back off a little. We're guarding nukes, you know—not a bunch of airplanes. They're not going to get up and fly away."

Vikki pointed at a dirt cutoff, barely visible in his headlights. "How about there?"

Britnell responded by slamming on the brakes. He switched off the lights and turned. He drove faster as his eyes grew accustomed to the dark. Sage and cactus scratched against the Bronco, making a din that nearly drowned out the engine. Vikki yelled over the bouncing.

"What about those sensors you showed me on that map—aren't you afraid of hitting them?"

Britnell patted the IFF. "When we get close to one, this baby will sing out. Don't worry—the worst that could happen is that we'll run over one and they'll send out a repair crew to fix it."

Vikki was slammed against her seat, then lifted suddenly into the air as they ricocheted over a mound. Britnell spun the Bronco around until they faced

Alpha Base. The lights were three miles away, but they still looked impressive.

Britnell turned off the engine. His eyes ran up and down Vikki's body. "How's this?"

"Perfect. It's just what I had in mind."

Britnell's eyes lit up. "Oh?"

She smiled coyly. "Let's play a game."

He wet his lips. "Sure. Sure."

"Give me your gun, and get undressed."

He started unbuttoning his shirt. "What?"

"Come on." She playfully pushed him against the side of the Bronco. "Your gun. You afraid, big guy?"

With his shirt halfway off, he handed her the pistol. "Be careful—"

Vikki giggled and ran the cold metal around his chest. She made tiny swirls, growing to ever larger circles. Leaning over, she gently kissed his neck. "How does that feel?"

"Weird. You know, with the gun . . ."

She laughed again. "Exciting, isn't it?"

Britnell finished taking off his shirt and started unbuckling his pants.

Vikki said gently, "That's it." Slowly she pushed his head forward, running the cold metal up his side. She set her mouth. The times he'd pawed her, thinking only of himself . . . he'd self-destruct on booze if he continued. She wouldn't have to do anything at all to make him kill himself. She felt a sudden twinge. *If something happened and the raid was called off, she wouldn't be implicated in his death.* Memories flooded through her.

She ran the gun up his neck. Britnell started to laugh. His head was underneath the steering wheel, his back parallel to the seat, and his chest was against his knees. With her free hand Vikki pulled Britnell's jacket over his head. "Hey, what's this?" he asked.

"Here's where it gets good, babe." Vikki brought the gun up and pulled quickly on the trigger. A blast filled the Bronco.

Britnell jerked, then was quiet. His arms went slack, and what was left of his head fell to the steering wheel.

Vikki reached over his body and opened the door. He tumbled out onto the desert. The Bronco was remarkably clean of carnage—the .22 drilled a neat hole into his skull, exiting the front of his head and leaving a gaping wound. His jacket absorbed most of the blood. Little evidence existed inside the jeep of Britnell's death.

Vikki coolly scooted to the driver's seat, swinging her legs over the stick shift. The key turned the engine over the first time she tried it. When she left, she didn't look back.

Vikki cut across the desert, heading east, away from Alpha Base and toward the runway. Moonlight dimly lit the concrete apron that was used to unload the nukes. Low-wattage orange "ready lights" splashed their glow on the ground. As expected, the apron was empty of any cargo planes.

Beyond the apron, Christmas-treelike lights demarcated the runway. A series of strobes flashed in a sequence, pointing toward the main landing strip.

Vikki slowed and drove around the concrete loading pad. She tried a direct line to the runway, but a faint warbling sound came from the IFF unit. A tiny red light flashed angrily on top of the unit.

Vikki slammed on the brakes. *The sensors—it's detecting a sensor.* The IFF cloaked her from radar, but the sensors would still pick up noise from the Bronco. She put the jeep into reverse and slowly backed up.

As she moved backward the warbling grew fainter

and the red light flickered off. She had left the detailed map of Alpha Base with Harding, but she could still make it to the hangar at the end of the runway by going slowly and using the IFF to catch the sensors before they detected her.

She headed north a hundred yards. Glancing at her watch, the digital readout flashed ten-fifty. *Ten minutes before Renault lands.* She turned the steering wheel back east and accelerated. On a hunch, she steered toward the runway—she now headed on a diagonal to her original path. Driving with one eye on the moonlit desert and the other on the IFF, she continued, slowly waiting for the sensor light to come on . . .

Wham! She looked wildly around. Her front tires hit the access road. The shock jolted her. She thought about flicking her lights on, but decided against it. The road was fairly well delineated, but she had to squint over the steering wheel to make sure she was still on track.

She rounded the runway, speeding past the strobe lights without passing anyone. Slowing she searched for the deserted aircraft hangar. She almost panicked when she couldn't find it, but when a patch of stars was suddenly blocked by its shape, she felt relieved.

Vikki slowed to a stop. She made out the moving van nestled against the hangar.

She turned off the engine and climbed out of the Bronco. No one was in sight. She wasn't surprised— Harding had to be sure that she was alone. She stood by the Bronco and waited.

A rustle came from her right. She started to turn— Someone grabbed her from behind. A hand covered her mouth and pulled her down. She tried not to cry out. Dirt and rock ground into her side.

"She's alone," hissed a voice. The hands released

her. She brushed herself off as Harding appeared in front of her.

By an elbow he drew her away from the men and looked her over. "Well?"

Vikki brushed herself off. "It's all set."

"Show me the IFF." Harding picked up a toolbox and lugged it with him.

They climbed inside the vehicle. Harding stuck his feet out the door so he could position himself under the IFF. If he saw any blood, he ignored it, concentrating instead on the radar cloaking device. Vikki pointed out the basic features as he asked questions.

Harding motioned for the toolbox and withdrew a socket wrench. Minutes later he pulled the IFF from its chassis. He turned it over and placed it on the seat.

"So that's it?"

"What did you expect?"

Harding squinted at his watch. "Any time now. You cut it close, Vikki. If you were any later, we would have gone on without you."

Vikki chose to ignore him. The repartee was getting tiresome. They had more important things to do.

Grabbing the IFF, Harding motioned for her to follow. They moved quickly to the hangar. Pulled up flush with the three-story building, the moving van blended in with the surroundings. The back was open. Most of the men were sprawled around the truck, their weapons loose by their sides.

For all the relaxed atmosphere, Vikki soon noticed that the men were arranged symmetrically around the truck, facing so that the entire runway and access road were covered. Most of them smoked, holding cigarettes in the cups of their hands as she had seen Harding do earlier in the night. Her first impression of them as a ragtag group of terrorists began to fade as their professional demeanor began to shine through.

As Harding approached, the men sprang easily to their feet. They gathered around as he spoke.

"I want everyone to keep hidden until Renault gets here. No one moves until I give the all-clear."

A faint droning interrupted him. Searching the night sky, Harding spotted the strobe and landing lights of the C-130. It came in from the west, its four propellers cutting through the air.

"All right, places everyone." Harding bolted to the moving van and gingerly placed the dismantled IFF on the front seat. He grabbed a rifle and reached into the van. "Vikki, are you armed?"

"Yeah—Britnell's pistol." It was missing one bullet, she thought.

Harding pulled out another rifle, smaller than the one he carried, and tossed it to her. "Use this instead. It's an automatic. Flip up the safety, but don't use more than single shots—you'll run out of bullets too fast if you don't."

Vikki caught the weapon and turned it over. The droning grew louder, escalating to a gut-wrenching roar. The men flattened against the hangar, hiding from any light directed their way.

Vikki moved over by Harding and watched. The C-130 was clearly visible now. Its wheels bounced on the long runway, landing at the midpoint. Smoke shot out from where the wheels hit the asphalt. The engines reversed, slowing the transport and sending a thunder of prop wash across the field. They'd find out soon if the call signs Britnell provided them worked.

The plane kept moving. As it drew closer, Vikki could make out the dim cockpit lights. The crew inside the aircraft gave no indication that they could see the moving van or hangar.

"Come on, come on." Harding clenched his rifle tighter.

The C-130 drew abreast of them. Slowing, it rotated in a hairpin turn, back toward the taxiway. As it turned, the rear compartment opened, splitting wide, looking like an alligator's mouth. The loading ramp bounced as it hit the ground. The C-130 stopped briefly, and a dark vehicle emerged from the gaping hole.

The APC! Vikki ran over the APC's characteristics in her head: lightweight and agile, it could reach speeds of over forty-five miles per hour, and yet carry ten men and their weapons to just about any target. Powered by an array of batteries, the APC made virtually no sound. As it sped toward them, the camouflaged aluminum skin gave the APC a dull finish.

The C-130 pulled away, moving back down the runway as it closed its ramp.

Harding jumped up and ran toward the APC. With the plane departing to the opposite end of the runway, the APC's small size surprised Vikki—filling the C-130's cargo bay, it gave the optical illusion that the vehicle was monstrous.

Harding directed the APC to the van. A hatch opened at the top of the vehicle. Renault pushed his head through the opening. "Glad to see everyone made it to the party."

Harding slipped over and jumped nimbly onto the vehicle. "Stop screwing around and open the back compartment."

Renault met his glare and nodded. A low whine came from the APC after Renault ducked down in the innards. The APC's back end lifted open.

Harding glanced at his watch, then called out, "Get a move on. We've got a little less than half an hour."

Four men transferred boxes of plastique to the Bronco; the one called Pablo Jaqueratee was in charge. They loaded the rear section high, then piled into the vehicle with their rifles. Colonel Renault spoke to the group before waving Harding and Vikki over.

"The communications squad is heading out. Are you going to have any trouble installing the IFF unit?"

Harding shook his head. "Not any more difficulty than putting in a cassette recorder. I'll hook it up to the battery and run the antenna through the hatch."

"So we can still go by our original schedule?"

"Unless something happens to the helicopter squad, we'll go as planned."

"Good." Renault turned back to the Bronco and gave final instructions to the men. "Pablo—after you're done, head off base. No one will stop you in the confusion." They nodded, then started off. Vikki backed away from the Bronco as it left. Harding and Renault conferred for a moment before Harding broke away for the moving van.

"Vikki, I want you to operate the IFF. You're the only one with experience."

"What experience?"

"You used it getting here, didn't you?"

She nodded.

Harding retrieved the IFF from the moving van and started installing it as the men finished loading the APC. For the first time since the night activities began, Vikki felt a chill. Then she realized her bra felt uncomfortable—she hadn't noticed it until she'd let her mind wander.

Renault gathered the remainder of the men around him. Ten would be in the armored personnel carrier with Vikki, Harding, and Renault, crowding the APC; thirty-six men were with the helicopter team, still in the back of the C-130; and the four men in the Bronco rounded out the list. Fifty-three people against four times that many stationed on Alpha Base.

But they had the element of surprise—they knew what they would be doing next; the personnel on Alpha Base wouldn't know what hit them.

Vikki shivered from a sudden gust of cool wind. Swinging up onto the APC, she took a final glance around before dropping her rifle down into the hatch.

Her ears still rang from the C-130's close passing. She thought she could still make out the engine's droning.

She hesitated. The plane should have been long gone by now.

She *heard* something. "Anthony. *Anthony!*"

Harding stuck his head up through the hatch. "What?"

Vikki pointed to the access road. A pair of headlights bore straight toward them. The sound she heard moments before cascaded. "We've got visitors."

2238 local

Inside the C-130

The APC's electric motor whirred into motion as the C-130 turned away from the deserted hangar. The cargo ramp hit the runway with a thump, bouncing as the APC roared down the ramp.

Once the APC exited, the ramp lifted and fit smoothly onto the back of the C-130 tail section. Frank Helenmotz pushed forward to the cockpit. Wendover's runway stretched out in front of him. The lights lining the runway seemed to go on forever.

The lights brought back the memories. Since meeting Colonel Renault, Helenmotz got to fly nearly all he wanted. He was checked out in so many helicopters, he'd lost count. Everything from British Westland Commandos to Soviet Mi-24 Hinds.

And the beauty was that Renault paid him. Doing all the dirty little jobs that a country itself could not afford to be connected with. It was a good life: in the army without the army bullshit.

Helenmotz squinted through the darkness and made out a score of lumps parked by the side of the runway. One of the lumps was lit well enough to see—an HH-53 helicopter squatted on the asphalt, its blades almost touching the ground. An auxiliary power unit stood just inside the perimeter of light. The soft glow of two cigarettes pinpointed the technicians responsible for keeping the helicopter on alert.

As the C-130 taxied down the runway, Helenmotz nudged the pilot. The man, also a member of Renault's legion, slid his headset down around his neck. Helenmotz shouted over the din, "Swing closer to the helicopters."

The pilot shook his head. "Too risky. We're being tracked by the ground control."

"You don't have to run the helicopters over—just get closer to them. Thirty-six men are depending on you not to blow their cover."

"I've got my own cover to worry about. What the hell do you think they're going to do if they find out I'm not from Peterson Field?"

Helenmotz glanced out the cockpit window. "Don't worry about it—just get us close to the helicopters."

"What will I tell the tower?"

"I don't know. You figure it out. Tell them you lost hydraulic pressure on one of your rudders or something. And don't forget to slow down when you get there."

The pilot ignored him and straightened the headset on his ears. Helenmotz waited momentarily to see if the man would listen to him. When the aircraft swerved toward the helicopters, Helenmotz hurried to the cargo bay. They had to hurry—the C-130 from Peterson AFB would be here in the next twenty minutes.

The men sat alert on the webbed seating, rifles on their knees. Their entire focus was on capturing the helicopters and flying into Alpha Base. Helenmotz jerked his head toward the jump master door at the rear of the craft.

"Let's get a move on—when the 130 slows, get the hell out of here. The choppers will be directly in front of you. One more time: set the timers for 2300 and make sure the *last* five choppers on the right are clean. I don't want anybody's chopper blowing up because one of you nippleheads got too enthusiastic. Got it?"

Grim faces stared back at him.

"All right—let's go."

Helenmotz scooted to the side and started handing out satchels. Five to a man. Helenmotz opened the top bag and did a random check: five pounds of plastique explosive, a timer, and a fuse. He slapped the satchel shut. Twenty-five pounds of explosives for each man—more than enough to take out the helicopters in the Wendover fleet.

Helenmotz pushed his way to the rear. Laying down the explosives, he struggled with the jump master door. A red light burned above the door, signifying "don't jump."

Dry air spilled into the C-130 when the hatch swung open. JP-4 and diesel fuel raced through his nostrils. The HH-53 parking area was to his left and coming up fast. The C-130's engines seemed to back off a bit, and the craft actually slowed. The pilot tapped the brakes and the craft slowed further.

Helenmotz jerked his head at the hatch. "Get ready—he may not have a chance to stop. I'll go first."

He looked down at the runway whizzing by and tried to judge the speed. A parachute-landing fall would be a piece of cake; but if he jumped out now, he'd risk landing on the satchel. He decided that falling on twenty-five pounds of explosives wasn't too swift an idea.

The C-130 turned slightly. Helenmotz wet his lips and squinted at the runway. It was hard to tell how fast they were going, but dammit, they didn't have much time left. The pilot was being too careful, not slowing any further, so Helenmotz decided they had to go. He drew in a deep breath and leaped out of the craft.

He landed running, nearly tripped, and caught himself. Slowing to a jog, he crouched and waited for the others to exit. One after another the thirty-five men leaped from the C-130.

The plane seemed to linger too long after they egressed. Helenmotz waited. He wondered if the pilot even knew that they had jumped. If he stays any longer, he'll draw attention to us, he thought.

The C-130 turned a wing away from the row of helicopters and revved its engines. Helenmotz silently cursed the pilot, hoping he hadn't blown their cover. He decided to wait a moment more before heading out.

Nothing stirred around the HH-53's. It was a dead Saturday night—no activity that might detect them. He couldn't see the security policemen guarding the flight line, but his men would take care of them.

He started for the helicopters. The men trailed him,

each silently waiting to secure their satchels underneath the helicopters—and then to board a chopper for the assault on Alpha Base.

2240 local

Wendover AFB Command Post

"Sir, they've landed."

"What?" Major McGriffin struggled up in his seat. His professional military education lay on the floor, open to a chapter entitled *Canals and Interstates: America's Strategic Byways.* He rubbed at his eyes. "Who landed?"

"Merry Zero Three, sir," reminded Staff Sergeant Salanchez. The communications tech nodded toward the status board. "The reserve unit out of Peterson Field. They landed thirty minutes early. You wanted us to wake, er, I mean notify you when the C-130 arrived from Colorado Springs. Something about one of your classmates being on board?"

"Oh, yeah." McGriffin stretched. "Thanks, I'll check in with them." He picked up a cup of decaf sitting on his desk and took a sip.

The coffee was cold. He forced a swallow and jammed the cup back on the desk. Yawning, he scratched and twisted his neck, taking in the command post. All the ready boards were green. Even the "threat condition" sign burned green with THREATCON ALPHA.

McGriffin called out to Salanchez, "Can you get base ops on the line?"

The sergeant punched at the phone. "Line five one, Major—I'm ringing now."

McGriffin picked up the telephone. "Yeah, this is Major McGriffin over at the CP. Have you got a roster on that 130 from Pete—Merry Zero Three?" A moment passed. "Well, do you know if they'll be filing a flight plan to return?" Another moment . . . "That's odd. When do they plan to rotate?" McGriffin threw a glance at the clock. "Okay. Thanks."

He hung up and stared at the desk. Chief Zolley moved to his side.

"What's up, sir?"

"Huh? Oh, nothing. Nothing." McGriffin turned and folded his arms. He picked up a pencil and tapped it sporadically on the desk; turning back to Zolley, McGriffin played with the pencil's eraser. "Chief, something doesn't seem right."

"What do you mean, sir?" Zolley perched on the side of the desk and took a sip of his coffee.

"I'm not sure. I may be completely off base on this, but it seems peculiar that a plane would come all the way from Colorado Springs, not remain overnight, and take off again."

"Yes, sir."

McGriffin sprang up from his seat and paced in front of the desk. "If I hadn't known so many wild 130 flyers, I'd think nothing of it. Those guys are always on the prowl, and since they're a reserve unit, they've signed up to do this sort of thing: go on temporary duty and party. It doesn't make sense they would just leave." He called out to the communications unit. "Salanchez—get base ops at Pete Field on AUTOVON. Find out if they've got a C-130, call sign Merry Zero Three, filed for Wendover—"

"The call sign checks out, sir," interrupted Zolley.

"Checks out with whom?"

"With the weekly list, sir."

"And not necessarily with what left Pete Field." McGriffin placed a hand on the back of his chair.

"What are you saying, sir?" said Zolley slowly.

"Did you ever see *A Gathering of Eagles,* Chief?" Frowning, Zolley shook his head no. "I must have seen that thing a hundred times at the Academy—they were always pumping us full of that Air Force rah-rah bull during Basic summer. Anyway, there's a spot in that movie where the wing commander loses his job because of an Operational Readiness Inspection. He wasn't prepared for what the readiness team threw at him." McGriffin nodded his head. "I'll bet ten to one that's what SAC has done. They're throwing us a ringer—probably got an ORI set up to catch us napping."

"Major McGriffin." Staff Sergeant Salanchez stood and held a hand over the receiver.

"Yes?"

"Sir, Peterson Field says no C-130 from there is anywhere near Wendover."

"Are they sure?"

"Absolutely. They had planned a sortie and even scheduled an arrival time of 2300, but they're having a freak snowstorm and all of their birds are grounded."

McGriffin slammed a hand against the back of his chair. The command post grew quiet at the exchange. He nodded to Salanchez. "Thanks, Sergeant; I remember it *can* snow in June there." He turned to Zolley. "Well, what do you think?"

"I kind of like your Operational Readiness Inspection idea, sir. But if the 130 said it's from Pete Field—and yet Pete doesn't know anything about it . . ." He trailed off.

"Yeah," said McGriffin. He spun the chair around and plopped down in the seat. Drumming his fingers on the desk, he suddenly asked Zolley, "Did base ops get a look at the tail number on that 130?"

Chief Zolley's brows lifted. "They didn't say. Good idea, sir." A minute later he put the phone down. "They can't see anything. He took a long roll on landing, then when he taxied, lingered near the helicopter apron. When he refueled, it looked like he was all black—he insisted he could refuel for only fifteen minutes before leaving, too. He's just been cleared for takeoff."

McGriffin closed his eyes. "All black. It could be a Blackbird—one of the special ops birds at Hurlburt; but those guys still play by the rules." He opened his eyes and swiveled around. "Any chance it could have been something out of Tonopah?"

If the command post was silent before, it was as lively as a morgue now. Tonopah was the highly classified air base a few hundred miles north of Las Vegas, rumored to house the Air Force's newest "black" programs—that's where the stealth fighters and bombers started out, and other things that the Air Force never admitted existed.

Zolley slowly shook his head. "No way, Major. We *always* get advance notice about anything from there coming our way. We lock the runway up so tight, not even the rattlesnakes can get in or out."

McGriffin threw a glance at the clock. "They're cleared to take off in five minutes—maybe I should raise Colonel DeVries . . ." He trailed off.

Just having a plane land and take off was nothing to get excited about. So why should he worry?

Because of Alpha Base.

Wendover might be hicksville compared to Tacoma, but Wendover AFB had a heck of a lot more dangerous "assets."

"Chief, have base ops call the 130 back. I want to ask them some questions."

Zolley spoke up once he raised the tower. "The aircraft refuses to acknowledge them, Major. There is incoming traffic, two jets on final, coming up in the next four minutes—the 130 is cleared to roll after the jets land."

McGriffin drew in a breath. *Five minutes. The command post is right on the runway—a staff car could race out to the taxi pad and get a visual on the tail number in two minutes. There's plenty of time.*

He made up his mind. "Chief—you've got the command post while I'm gone. Keep in contact with me at all times—I'll take one of the walkie-talkies."

"You'll have to use an open channel, Major. The secure units are on the blink."

"What else could go wrong?" No one answered the rhetorical question. "All right, I'll use the jeep radio." The clock blinked, showing four minutes until takeoff. "Contact the helicopter squadron—tell them about the C-130 loitering around their apron, and have one of their guys meet me out there. I'm off."

As they cycled the door, he remembered leaving his hat on the desk. He fleetingly remembered a horse's rear colonel chewing him out in front of the base gym when he had failed to put on his hat—McGriffin had thought at the time: you command what you know. Wearing a hat had been a big deal then.

Now he didn't even think about going back to get it.

15

Wendover AFB

Harding ducked into the personnel carrier. He instantly popped back up with two rifles. He tossed one of them to Vikki. "Get the hell out of here. Cover the APC." He yelled down inside the personnel carrier: "Punch out the back. We've got visitors."

He pushed Vikki off the vehicle. She tumbled against the side and managed to land on her feet. She started to curse him, but realized that if they were fired upon, the APC would draw bullets like a magnet.

Keeping low to the ground, Vikki sprinted to a small depression. Crouching, she brought her rifle up and swiveled toward the approaching headlights.

In the dark the APC appeared as just another murky object. The headlights scared her. Maybe it's just a random check, she thought. If it were a full-scale attempt to stop us, all hell should have broken loose.

Unless Britnell hadn't told her everything.

She grew suddenly chilled at the thought. What if Britnell hadn't played straight with her—what if he'd been leading her on, gathering snips of information, and dealing with the brass on Wendover? What if they knew about all the information she had gotten from Britnell—the map?

She dismissed the thought. Britnell had been too open, too vulnerable with her—she *knew*. Besides, he couldn't have found out their plans.

Vikki grasped her weapon tightly and followed the headlights through the gun sight.

A minute passed . . . as the lights grew closer, she heard music blaring from the vehicle. The car weaved down the road, screeching to a halt fifty feet from the APC. Laughter, clinking bottles, and smells of pot and liquor drifted from the car.

Vikki brought the rifle down. *Kids!*

Saturday night was international date night, and Wendover AFB was not excluded, especially from military brats. Vikki relaxed. *If those damn kids would only get the hell out of here* . . .

The laughter grew louder as car doors opened. ". . . I got to take a whiz. I'll be right back." A figure staggered to the hangar. Vikki peered through the darkness. She made out the features of two girls and a boy in the car. *Two couples.* It could have been her, twenty years ago, on a double date back in Colorado. . . .

A teenager's voice called from the hangar. "Hey, look at this!" The laughter in the car abated.

"Hurry up. We don't have all night."

"A moving van—holy cow, it's an abandoned party wagon!"

The hilarity inside the car increased. The occupants spilled out and picked themselves up. Weaving to the van, they met their compatriot. They wandered around the van, inspecting the cab and giggling in low whispers.

"Oh, wow. I don't believe it—"

"Do." Colonel Renault and ten of his men materialized in front of the kids, weapons leveled.

"Oh, shit." One of the teenagers wavered.

"Not another word from any of you." Renault waved his rifle at the two couples. "Climb inside the back of the truck. Move it."

The men opened ranks and formed a conduit to the moving van. They roughly pushed the kids up inside. One of the girls started sobbing.

"Shut up," snarled Renault.

The teenager who first climbed out of the car picked himself up and nursed an injured elbow. "Hey, what the hell do you sky cops think you're doing? Roughing us up—who do you think you are?"

Renault floored the youngster with his rifle butt. He glared at the rest of them and jumped from the van. Crying came from inside.

Vikki ran up just as Harding arrived. She brushed back her hair, then looped it back into a knot so it wouldn't get in the way. "Tie them up and get the hell out of here. We're running late."

Renault remained silent. He looked at Harding.

Harding narrowed his eyes. "Well?"

"Your call, Dr. Harding. Ms. Osborrn is right. We're starting to cut it close. We can't afford to wait around here any longer."

Harding wet his lips. Even in the dark Vikki could tell that his face was flushed. "Let's get going. We've come too far to back down."

Vikki turned to one of Renault's men. "Tie up the kids and get back to the APC."

The man didn't budge. "Colonel?"

Renault raised his brows at Harding. "Well?"

Harding nodded, seemingly oblivious to Vikki's presence. He whispered, "Get rid of them."

Vikki put an edge to her voice. She addressed Renault's men again. "You heard him, tie them up—"

"I *said,* get rid of them."

"What!" Vikki looked incredulous.

Harding stared down Vikki. "We can't let a bunch of damn kids ruin this."

"What the hell are you talking about, Anthony? You've got four kids in that van, crapping in their pants—scared out of their wits we're going to kill them. If we tie them up, there's no way they're going to get loose in less than an hour. By then we'll be smack in the middle of Alpha Base—"

Harding cut her off with a wave. "And what happens if in two minutes after we leave they're found by a security police patrol? We can't afford to screw up."

"But these are just kids . . ."

"What's more important, dammit? This operation or a couple of kids' lives?" Harding whirled and pointed at Renault. "Get rid of them." He stomped off toward the APC.

Vikki stood in a daze. She couldn't believe her ears. It was one thing for her to kill Britnell—the poor slob didn't deserve to live, the way he'd leeched off her; but killing four kids?

Twenty years ago it could have been her.

The girls must have been shot first, because it was a male scream that pierced the dark.

She walked numbly to the personnel carrier. Men rushed past her, climbing back into the APC through the back access.

Renault passed her, then slowed, allowing her to catch up. He pulled on a short cigarette. "Welcome to the club, Ms. Osborrn." She didn't answer. Renault continued, "Dr. Harding's decision to kill those kids was just as hard as yours to kill that airman earlier tonight. Don't damn him because of it."

"But that security police fascist *deserved* to die—"

"*Nobody* deserves to die, Ms. Osborrn. So don't go playing God. That airman wasn't some roach you step on, grinding out of existence without a thought. People kill for different reasons—because the victim 'deserves to die' isn't one of them. On my team, my men kill because I tell them."

"What about you, Colonel? Why do you kill?" Vikki asked coolly.

Renault threw his cigarette down and ground it out with a heel. "I kill for money, so I guess that makes me a capitalist. What's your excuse?"

He unshouldered his rifle and walked faster, leaving her behind him.

Vikki drew in several breaths. Reaching the APC, she swung up, adrenaline pumping her full of new-found energy. She tossed her rifle to the men inside. "Let's get the hell out of here. We've got a crater full of nukes waiting."

Sealing the hatch above her, she wiggled to a free spot. Renault squeezed in the driver's compartment. She ignored him.

Renault flipped up the television screen. The ground around them glowed an eerie hue, shown as black-on-white contrast from infrared sensors mounted outside the APC. Piped in through optic fibers, the IR imaging highlighted everything around the APC for hundreds of yards.

Vikki watched the IR screen as Renault started off across the desert. He kept away from the access road and other hot spots showing up on the screen. Harding tapped her on the shoulder.

"Do you want to man the IFF?"

"Sure." Vikki exchanged places with him. Sitting that close to Renault had made her self-conscious. Moments before, he had struck at a nerve she couldn't quite define.

The Identification Friend or Foe unit kept her busy, making the trip to Alpha Base seem shorter. Harding crammed next to Renault, listening to Alpha Base radio frequencies.

Vikki looked over Renault's shoulder at the map Britnell had given her. She spoke up. "We're entering the active zone, five miles from Alpha Base."

Renault replied without looking at her. "Just keep us away from the sensors and we'll worry about everything else."

A light on the IFF flickered faintly. "Try heading north," Vikki said. Renault responded instantly. The light on the IFF disappeared.

Harding turned and shot her a glance. She couldn't read his eyes—they were still glazed from the killing he had ordered not five minutes ago. Vikki set her mouth. She was still in this—she hadn't changed her views. Renault had reminded her of that. But she wondered if Harding had changed, and what he was doing this for.

2242 local

Wendover AFB

McGriffin ground the jeep's transmission as he tried to shift into second. Finally finding the gear, he immediately changed to third. He blasted away from the command post and sped toward the flight line.

Cutting across a parking lot, he bypassed the loop that normally would have taken him on a path running by base operations.

He flipped on the jeep radio and tried to raise the command post while driving with one hand. "CP, this is Mobile One—can you get me cleared for the flight line?"

Chief Zolley's voice came over the airwaves. "Roger that, Mobile One. They'll be keeping an eye out for you. The security police will provide an escort. Do you wish to call an on-base emergency at this time?"

McGriffin ran a stop sign. Punching the accelerator, he sped on through the intersection, just missing a Ford Bronco. Calling an on-base emergency would be the equivalent thing to calling an in-flight emergency if he were flying. Basically, the crap would hit the fan and he'd have immediate, unqualified support from all units on base. And everybody and his brother breathing down his neck.

McGriffin keyed the microphone. "Hold that call, Chief. But if anything happens, then don't hesitate hitting the panic button."

McGriffin steered past the helicopter squadron. Bursting across the invisible boundary that delineated the parking pad from the apron, McGriffin shot onto the taxiway.

He threw the microphone in the passenger seat and grasped the steering wheel. If he'd been on an operational flying base, he'd have been spotted by now, challenged by an M-16–toting security policemen who guarded the birds on the flight line. As it was, he was all alone except for an escort that should be catching up with him.

He didn't have to worry about hitting an aircraft— they'd be so brightly lit it would be impossible to miss.

Once on the active runway, he wouldn't have to worry about colliding with one of the helicopters.

The C-130 sat at the end of the runway, a mile and a half away.

A jet screamed overhead—a T-38 supersonic trainer—followed by another. They pulled a landing, greasing onto the runway with hardly a bounce. McGriffin guessed they were instructors from one of the undergraduate pilot training bases, off on a night-time cross-country mission.

The C-130's engines roared. It started moving. McGriffin continued to race down the runway. He kept far to the edge, careful not to stray close to the lumbering craft. He needed to check the tail number, but he wasn't stupid.

The C-130 roared past, its red taillight faintly illuminating the vertical stabilizer. McGriffin squinted through the darkness. The tail was painted black. He couldn't see any numbers or identifying marks. As the plane receded from him, McGriffin downshifted and watched it lift into the air.

Something struck him. The C-130 was stretched, longer than the typical TAC birds. He wasn't sure if the special ops planes were stretched or not. He hit the steering wheel as he drew to a stop.

"Great." Fumbling for the radio, McGriffin keyed the mike. "Command Post, this is Mobile One. I couldn't get a visual on them."

"That's a rog, Mobile One." A security police car pulled up beside him, lights flashing. Two armed enlisted men decked out in their camouflaged battle-dress uniforms stepped from the car. McGriffin quickly spoke into the radio. "Chief, you got a positive ID on my actions out here, don't you?"

"Yes, sir. We gave the SP's everything but the code

words, which we could not say over open channels. Is there anything wrong?"

"I don't think so. In any case, I'll be heading back as soon as I'm through. Stand by." He looked up at the security policemen.

They saluted. "Evening, sir. Can we see an ID?" They stood warily back. One of them held his M-16 at a ready angle.

"Sure." McGriffin returned their salute and pulled out his green military identification card.

One of the men studied it then handed it back. "We got a request to escort a command post vehicle out to the flight line, Major. The NCOIC wants to know what the hell—sorry, sir—what in the world is going on."

McGriffin pocketed his card. "Nothing now, I'm afraid. We were just following up on something hot."

McGriffin slumped against the back of his seat and looked up at the stars. Wheeling high overhead, they burned bright in the crisp night.

The sergeant jerked his head at his partner, then turned back to McGriffin. "You'll have to follow us off the flight line, sir."

"What? Sure." McGriffin straightened in his seat. Things still didn't seem right. He knew what he should do: head back to the CP and find out what in the heck was going on. *No bombs bursting in air, no ORI—everything is calm. Except for that activity near the chopper squadron, the C-130 might never have been here.* It didn't make sense. He picked up the microphone. "Are you still there, Chief?"

"Yes, sir. Everything all right?"

"Salubrious and copacetic." He had a sudden twinge in his gut; might as well combine pleasure with business, he thought. "Chief, I'm going to swing by the chopper squadron and check things out, then hit the Hole in the Ground before coming back. Want me to bring back a grease burger?"

"You know how I feel about those things, sir."

"Right. I promise to finish eating it before I get back." He clicked off and looked up to the security policemen. "Mind if we head out by the chopper squadron? Base ops reported some activity near there."

"If you want, Major, but we've already checked it out."

"I'd like to see for myself."

The security policeman shrugged. "Whatever you want, sir."

As they drove off, McGriffin whistled, his mind racing, wondering about the mysterious C-130. His stomach growled, turning his mind away from the problem at hand. Beef Stroganoff an AAFES burger was not, but at least it was nearby.

2242 local

Wendover AFB

Pablo Jaqueratee gripped the Bronco's steering wheel. Colonel Renault was a stickler for details. And because the colonel scrutinized the little things, his men carried out their instructions with zeal.

Pablo intently watched the road and turned at the cutoff. The other three members of the team quietly went over the map in their heads as well. If he took a wrong turn, he would be quickly admonished and set straight as to where he was heading.

He slowed for an intersection. A jeep squealed through a stop sign. Pablo watched the vehicle head off, then proceeded through the intersection.

He finally reached the building Renault had carefully pointed out to them. Antennas pricked the top of the low-slung building. Jaqueratee recognized the antennas from his past work in communications: ultra-high frequency, extremely high frequency, very low frequency. A satellite dish and microwave relay, both anchored to the roof, sat beside the antennas.

The building didn't look penetrable. Thick glass covered what few windows it had, and bars poked through the openings. But then again, they didn't have to take the building. They just had to ensure they severed communications so the base was shut off from the rest of the world.

Jaqueratee parked by an old white Corvette, so he was away from the building but still in a position to see what was going on. He checked his watch and conferred quickly with the others in the Bronco. Another ten minutes. Jaqueratee sat back and picked his teeth. He chose the best spots to lay the explosives. The first satchel of explosives would go by the front entrance—directly under the sign that said WENDOVER AFB COMMAND POST.

16

The five miles to Alpha Base took ten minutes to traverse. Gunning the APC at speeds up to forty-five miles an hour, Vikki Osborrn navigated the crew to the nuclear weapons storage area. She kept her eyes glued on the IFF—every time it flashed, she barked an order to change direction.

Renault steered by an image projected from a forward-looking television camera mounted at the top of the personnel carrier. The image came back in ghostly white and gray contrast, as the infrared processing amplified the low light around them.

Bushes, ravines, cactus, and boulders all showed up in eerie outline. Every now and then a brilliant white splotch would bound across the screen as the APC disturbed a jackrabbit from its hole.

They crossed the narrow road leading to Alpha Base

and swung south. Harding studied Britnell's map and directed Renault back toward the picnic grounds outside of Alpha Base.

The base loomed in the background as a white shimmer, growing brighter with every minute. Periodically Renault switched the forward-looking camera off the ground and scanned Alpha Base. The screen automatically reconfigured to adjust for the base's bright glow. This is almost too easy, Vikki thought. There has to be something more to it.

She glanced down at the IFF. "Sensor!" Renault jerked the craft to the right. An instant later the light faded. Vikki waited until the flicker disappeared, then breathed, "All clear."

Renault steered back to his original path, not looking back. Vikki watched the IFF. She felt flushed, caught up in Renault's drive to Alpha Base. It was almost like a drug—a yearning to get out and *do* something. She felt ready.

Alpha Base grew brighter, until it dominated everything on the screen. Slowing to a stop, Renault switched the image from infrared to normal lighting.

The screen blinked. They stopped a quarter mile from the four fences circling Alpha Base. The storage facility lay sprawled in the crater, lights splashing down on every bunker—the five miles across the complex seemed to stretch on forever. To their right lay the main gate. The picnic area was directly in front of them.

Renault turned and struggled from the cramped seat. Standing, he wiped his hands on his pants. "All right, listen up—we're running behind." The admonishment was unnecessary; no one spoke. "Mortar squad, half your shells should take out the road to Alpha Base and be ready to hit any vehicles they'll throw at us. We want to prevent a counterattack. They won't be able to get a fix on you, so don't worry about being spotted—the APC will draw them out.

"Once you expend your mortars, fall back to the baseball diamond in the picnic area. Your helicopter is not going to stick around and wait for you. If you're not there, that's it. We're not a damned rescue unit—the nukes come first. So if you want to get back alive, make sure you're there. Any questions?"

Renault looked around the APC. Most men kept their gaze fixed to the floor. Renault glanced at his watch. "All right, move it. Six minutes."

He turned back to the control panel and jabbed at the screen. The monitor reconfigured itself in a flash of red and blue. Renault pressed the touch-sensitive display and the rear ramp whirred open. Vikki sat back and watched the men hand out boxes of mortar shells and rifles. The whole process took less than two minutes.

When they finished, the mortar team dispersed. Renault closed the ramp and turned to Vikki and Harding. "Ready?"

Vikki set her mouth. "What now?"

"We wait. Two and a half minutes. And then we go."

2252 local

Wendover Command Post

Pablo Jaqueratee let his eyes dwell on the clock before it hit him: *ten fifty-two—eight minutes!* He struggled upright in the driver's seat. Punching the man next to him, he grunted, not speaking lest someone near the

151

Bronco might overhear them. The colonel had warned them about the various motion and sound sensors around Alpha Base—nothing prevented the Americans from planting sensors over the rest of the base.

The men stirred. Motioning with his hands, Pablo directed the others to shoulder their satchels of explosives.

A minute had transpired: *2253*.

Pablo eyed the command post. The satellite and microwave antennas were easy to destroy. The structures were relatively unhardened against anything more than a high wind.

The short, needle-thin, extremely high frequency antennas covered the building, looking like prickly pears. Optical phone lines ran from the building and plunged underground, intertwining with the other optical fibers connecting all base communications. They were buried, but a five-pound explosive tossed down the access hole would prevent any signals from leaving Wendover.

Stupid Americans, thought Pablo. Colonel Renault was right. They pay out the nose to harden their expensive equipment against all sorts of nuclear electromagnetic pulse, but totally discount a strike in their own backyard.

He checked the clock again: *2254*.

Pablo nodded for the men to disperse. Shifting the weight of the explosives higher on his shoulder, he grabbed the blanket from underneath his feet and slipped from the van. Once the men were out, they silently split up and went to their various stations.

Pablo raced to the barbed wire. He tossed the blanket on top of the ten-foot-high fence and scaled it.

By the time he was on top of the roof, it was 2256. *Four minutes.* He set the timer, gave it a quick pat, and peeled out.

2252 local

Wendover AFB Flight Line

Frank Helenmotz moved from one helicopter to another. The choppers weren't hangared, but left out in the open. As Helenmotz ran, the cool desert air blew through his open shirt, rippling against his flesh. Any other night he would have been chilled.

Tonight he sweated.

Helenmotz's men had dragged the bodies of five security policemen into the shadows. The pad was isolated, ideal for setting up the charges and hot-wiring the helicopters for their assault. Except for a jeep driving past every few minutes, and the guards out by the end of the taxiway, Helenmotz and his men were left alone. He couldn't have asked for anything better.

But things weren't going right at all.

Helenmotz personally supervised the installation of the first three explosives, checking the wires and ensuring the timers were set for 2300.

After they wired the third helicopter, things started going wrong.

He heard a "plunk" as he waved the men on, splitting them up to set the rest of the explosives. The alert bird—a helicopter kept ready to instantaneously fly away in case of an emergency—sat well away from the ones they scurried about.

But the "plunk" sounded bad.

Helenmotz ducked down and raced back to the

153

giant HH-53. Looming over him like a silent sleeping giant, Helenmotz crawled under the 53's fuselage. The explosive had fallen from the airframe, jarring the timer away from the fuse. Great, he thought. If he hadn't found it, it wouldn't have exploded.

Helenmotz slapped the fuse and timer together before setting the explosive back underneath the fuselage. He decided this was the optimal place— hiding it inside the chopper would draw too much attention if it were found.

He placed the plastique underneath the body, right by the wheel well. It was virtually impossible to see.

Helenmotz crawled out from under the chopper and decided to inspect the other two helicopters.

Both explosives had fallen from their places. One had the timer and fuse still together, the other was separated.

Helenmotz cursed and fixed the two. He had a sudden thought—racing back to the first chopper, he saw what he was looking for. He swore to himself. The explosive had fallen again.

He ran his hand over the fuselage. The skin felt cold to his touch. Something was wrong. If this wasn't an aluminum skin, then what was it? It felt like plastic. But it *had* to be aluminum—what the hell else could it be?

More important, all the plastique planted by the men were probably no longer sticking to the helicopters.

He glanced at his watch: *2256—four minutes and the show begins.* Wetting his lips, he looked hurriedly around. He spotted one or two of the men slipping in among the helicopters. Too little time was left to ensure that all the HH-53's would blow. If they didn't . . .

Helenmotz angrily pushed the thought out of his

mind. It was too late to prevent what happened—he had to move on to the next part of the plan: load the men!

He ran across two rows of helicopters. Four of his men disappeared around a helicopter. Moments later they trotted up to him. "That's it."

Helenmotz grunted. They had to time it right— after the communications building blew, but before the plastique they planted went off. When they started the chopper's engines, the sound would draw security policemen like a shark feeding frenzy. With Pablo's diversion at the command post they might be able to get the five choppers off the ground.

He glanced at his watch again: *2258*. Two minutes. He directed the men to load the choppers. Swinging up into the cockpit, he ran his hands over the equipment. In the darkness he managed to find his way around without too much difficulty.

A light glinted off the windshield. Jerking his head up, he caught sight of two cars moving slowly up to the helicopters. The first was a jeep; the other was a security police car. Men climbed from the cars.

2257 local

Wendover AFB Flight Line

McGriffin pulled up to the flight line. Although the two security policemen escorted him, he still felt wary about crossing the "drop dead" line encircling the HH-53's. He wasn't sure how serious they took the line at Wendover. He looked for the grim-faced security policemen guarding the line with an M-16 in hand—but no one was around. He knew that on a Saturday night the average nineteen-year-old guard would rather be doing quite a few other things besides pacing alone outdoors; but still, where were they?

McGriffin turned off his lights and waited for the security policemen to park beside him. He jumped from the jeep as a third car drove up. A figure in a flight suit slammed the door.

"Major McGriffin?"

"Over here." *The voice sounded familiar . . .*

The security policemen joined McGriffin as the man approached. The man called out, "Hiya, Bill—"

"Manny, what the fat brings you out here?" McGriffin shook hands with the lanky chopper pilot.

Yarnez grinned and returned the security policemen's salute. "I should be the one to ask. I was just pulling alert when I got this frantic call from Chief Zolley. He said you were chasing some airplane around and were afraid something was going on with the 53's." He scratched and lifted his eyebrows at McGriffin.

"Yeah, I'm not sure what's going on myself. I just wanted to check out your helicopters to make sure nothing was wrong."

Manny spread his arms. "Satisfied?"

McGriffin frowned and looked around. "What about the guards?"

Manny scanned the area, then shrugged. "They're on patrol. What do you think they're doing?"

"All right, don't rub it in." He glanced at his watch: *2259.* "I tell you what—I still want to track them down. Afterward I'll buy you a grease burger and fill you in."

"It's a deal. Hole in the Ground? I'll meet you there." He threw a quick salute and left for his car.

"Sure." McGriffin headed wearily for the flight line. What a night, he thought. Thinking he should check in with Zolley, he turned back to his vehicle—

The explosives went off as he reached the jeep. Momentarily blinded, he groped for the radio. Helicopter blades screamed around him. Heavy fumes of JP-4 nearly bowled him over.

He managed to click on the mike. "Command post—can you read me?"

A helicopter exploded not a hundred feet away, knocking him against the door. Flames shot into the air. A boiling cloud of smoke and fires rolled over the flight line. Another helicopter exploded, blinding him. Over the hiss of the walkie-talkie Chief Zolley cried, ". . . the command post is under attack!"

17

Saturday, 18 June, 2300 local

Alpha Base

"Now!" Renault jabbed at the screen. The APC jumped, its electric engines pushing the vehicle to the limit. Harding leaned over Renault's shoulder and punched up the outside view. He turned the audio down, lowering the sound of explosions crashing in.

Mortars screamed into the night. The area rocked with white noise as the explosives detonated. Harding pointed excitedly at the screen.

"The barracks—they took out the barracks!"

Renault ignored Harding's excitement and instead concentrated on urging the personnel carrier forward. Vikki strained to see the screen. An entire building roared in flames. The enlisted barracks, she thought. How many of Britnell's buddies were trapped inside? An image of the first party Britnell took her to raced through her mind, the groupies, girlfriends, and wives. *How many widows did we make tonight?*

The APC flew over the outside perimeter road and bore straight for the fences. Another building went up in flames—the command post and security station. Trucks exploded, mixing with sporadic gunfire.

"It's like Pearl Harbor," shouted Harding. He slapped Renault on the back and turned to Vikki, grinning. "We caught them napping—we're going to do it!"

They bore down on the first fence. Renault drove on, gluing his eyes to the screen.

"Fifty yards, hold on!"

Twang!

"Gunfire—they see us!"

"I don't think they've spotted us—they're shooting blind."

Renault gripped the steering column. Entering the smoothed-over dirt buffer zone, they were right on top of the fences. "Come on, baby. Let's punch right through. Four in a row."

Vikki dropped her rifle. She held on to her seat with both hands.

Brooomph!

They hit the first fence. Vikki strained to see the diagnostics flashing on Renault's screen. They hit the ten-foot-high barrier at forty-five miles an hour. The armored personnel carrier ripped a hole and slithered through the opening as if it weren't even there.

"Hold on—" *Broooomph!* The second fence whipped past. Harding whooped. The APC slowed minutely, then picked up speed . . .

She started to hold her breath and—*broooomph!*— they were through the third fence. The outside view jumped on the screen, then died. *The video camera's hit!*

"Keep away from the sides!" yelled Renault. "This one's electric—"

"Brooooomp! The screen went dark. The APC kept moving, but the electric engines whined from the impact. Seconds later the APC turned nosedown as it dove into the crater. The inside lights flickered, then blinked out. The APC hit something *hard,* bounced, and jerked to a halt.

"Everybody out!" shouted Renault in the darkness. "It'll only be a matter of seconds until they've figured out what happened. Move it!"

Vikki struggled with her belt. Renault knocked her down as he scrambled past her, crawling up the hatchway. "Hey!" Falling to the floor, she lifted herself up on one elbow and patted around for her rifle.

Renault clamored out the hatch. The sound of gunfire and sirens roared through the opening. Harding stuck his head down. "Vikki, what's keeping you?"

She pushed up and started for the ladder. "Get moving. I can take care of myself."

Reaching the top of the ladder, she shoved her rifle out first. *Twang!* Gunfire peppered the vehicle. She pushed herself over and rolled down the side, hitting the caked sand. The air roared with noise—red-orange flames belched smoke where the barracks had been. Several vehicles burned, smoking with remnants of a fire.

A dull thudding pounded the area—dirt, screams, and explosions mixed with the mortars still hitting Alpha Base. The sound of helicopters grew louder. She crawled alongside the APC and peered around the edge. Fifty feet lower in the crater Renault and Harding kneeled before a bunker door. They affixed explosives to the portal, carefully stacking roll after roll of plastique around the detonator. Harding pushed in a set of wires. He looked wildly around. A half dozen men fanned out, providing cover and setting up mortars inside Alpha Base.

"Get the hell out of here—we're ready to blow. Thirty seconds!"

Vikki grew cold; a shot of adrenaline raced through her. She had to get out of the way—fifty feet wasn't nearly far enough. She half crawled, half ran to the left, parallel to the fence. Slipping, she picked herself up and sprinted the distance to another bunker. She clambered around the side and leaned against the dirt berm, gasping for breath. Her chest heaved from the run. *Any second now.* She steadied herself against her rifle.

A helicopter popped overhead, its blades kicking up dust. Vikki swung her rifle up and squinted at the craft through her sight. Is it one of theirs or ours? she thought.

At the same instant, a pair of headlights jumped behind her. She swung her rifle around.

Making a split decision, she pumped off five rounds into the jeep. Screams, tires squealing, and the roar of the helicopter's wash. The jeep ran into the dirt berm, its wheels spinning as it flipped over. The helicopter shot back up into the sky. She followed it with her rifle, still unsure if it was one that had been commandeered or not.

An explosion rocked the ground. Rocks rained from the sky.

Vikki drew in several breaths. She took a moment to get reoriented, then scrambled around the bunker. Mortars thudded in the distance, Renault's men keeping the Alpha Base forces at bay.

Vikki grasped her rifle and trotted for the bunker Harding had blown. Dust from the helicopter and explosion settled, leaving a fine powder of sand and debris. Renault and Harding moved toward the bunker. Vikki picked up her pace.

Halfway there, three helicopters thundered overhead. Vikki started for cover. Landing, the choppers hit the ground and bounced. Eight of Renault's men scrambled from each craft, fanning out. When the last man exited, the helicopters lifted into the air.

Vikki continued to the bunker. The helicopters patrolled the area. A man hung out the door of each chopper, spraying the ground with bullets. Explosions peppered the ground from hand grenades they tossed.

Vikki slowed to a trot as she approached Harding. The physicist kicked at the bunker.

"Damn it all to hell!"

"What's up?" Vikki was surprised how her words squeaked out. She was badly out of breath.

"There must be four inches of steel in this door." He turned angrily to Vikki. "I thought that toad Britnell told you there was nothing special about these plates. Two hundred fifty pounds of plastique should have cracked it open."

"So the kid didn't know his shit. Can't you blow the hinges off?"

"A thousand pounds of dynamite would only buckle four inches of steel. You screwed up, Vikki. No, *I* screwed up. I should have never trusted the information you got out of that twerp."

"Wait one damned minute," shrilled Vikki. "If you're going around pointing fingers, you sure the hell better not point fingers at me. After all, who got you that IFF unit? Who—"

"Hold it, *hold it.*" Renault stepped between them.

"In case you didn't notice, we're smack in the middle of a shootout. If we're lucky, we've got about an hour and a half before they get their act together and counterattack. We've cut them off from higher headquarters, but they'll find a way to get to us. We're safe for now, but we can't stay here forever. The choppers will provide us with cover, and the rest of my men are combing the bunkers for stragglers."

He scanned the sky. "But we've got to hurry—my men didn't get all the helicopters. There may be some left back at the main Wendover complex."

Harding stepped unsteadily forward. *"What in the hell—"*

"I said there *may* be some left; one or two at the most." Renault turned to a metal box imbedded in the side of the concrete bunker. "Right now we'd better figure out how to get into the bunkers."

Harding breathed hard but stepped up and studied the container. It was open, smashed in by one of Renault's men. He seemed to calm down, appearing puzzled. "If this is the way to get into the bunker, I've never seen anything like it before."

"Neither have I," said Renault. He pointed to the inside of the box. "There's no place for a key or combo. Just a glass eye."

"Okay—so what do we do?" Harding looked to Renault.

Vikki took a step back, cooling down. "How many do you think we're up against?"

Renault set his mouth. "If your information about Alpha Base is correct"—Vikki shot a glance at Harding, but he ignored her—"we must have killed two thirds of the men in the barracks—about 130 out of two hundred. We've confirmed at least thirty more dead, leaving forty still out in the crater."

Harding scowled. "So we outnumber them."

"Barely," Renault reminded him.

Vikki scanned the area after a burst of gunfire rang out. "What about reinforcements?"

"That's the hour and a half buffer we've got. Even if they can mobilize their entire security police force, they can only throw another two hundred men at us. Reinforcements from another base will take at least that long to get here."

"Only another two hundred men. Great. Just fucking great." Harding slammed a hand against the metal box.

"All right, cut the whining. If you're still in this, then shut up and start contributing. If all you're going to do is bitch, then get the hell out of here. I'll do it myself. Understand?"

Renault stared at Harding. They glared at each other, each refusing to budge.

Vikki stepped forward. "We've got an hour and twenty-nine minutes, Colonel. What do we do?"

Harding opened his mouth. Vikki ignored him and studied Renault's face. "Come on, Colonel—you're wasting time."

Renault tore his attention away from Harding. He seemed to collect himself. "My men have orders to bring any officers they capture to me. Once we get someone in command, we'll force him to open the bunker."

"How will he do that?" asked Vikki.

Renault picked up his rifle. "That's the officer's problem, not ours. But until we find one, we split up. Don't do anything stupid—just capture him. Remember why we're here—it's not to play John Wayne."

2301 local

Wendover AFB Flight Line

McGriffin picked himself up off the concrete. His teeth hurt and he couldn't see out of one eye. Touching a hand to his head, he winced and drew back blood. He pried his eyelid open.

Acrid smoke bellowed from half of the helicopters. Flames licked at their undersides. A dozen HH-53's lay crumpled on the apron. Sirens wailed in the distance, giving the night a surrealistic effect. Suddenly, engines screamed, revving up.

"The helicopters—they're taking off!" McGriffin looked wildly around. He stumbled toward the flight line.

The security police car was in front of him, its lights out. McGriffin ran up and yanked open the door. One of the security policemen tumbled out, his head lolling listlessly to the side. Blood dripped from his mouth and ears. McGriffin looked up as one of the helicopters lurched from the ground. The super Jolly Green Giant hovered in the air, slowly moving upward. It passed over him, spraying its wash across the area.

The other policeman didn't move. As a second helicopter lifted off the pad, McGriffin reacted. He pulled the .45-caliber pistol out of the dead security policemen's holster, then unlocked the back door to the police car. Grabbing the shotgun from its holder in the rear window, McGriffin crouched low as the second helicopter passed over him.

McGriffin's brain yammered at him: *They're stealing the helicopters!* It seemed crazy—setting off explosions, attacking the command post—

The command post! Chief Zolley had shouted something about the command post being attacked when the explosions started.

McGriffin pushed past the security policeman's body and grabbed for the microphone. He clicked it. "CP, this is Mobile One. Come in CP." No response. "Anybody, come in!" He threw the mike back inside the car and stood.

The whining continued. A third helicopter started to lift—

A hand touched McGriffin's shoulder. He whirled, bringing the shotgun up to Manny Yarnez's face.

"Whoa—it's only me." Manny backed away and held his hands up, his eyes open wide.

McGriffin put the shotgun down. "Manny. Are you all right?"

Manny rubbed the back of his neck. "Yeah, I guess. What about these guys . . ." His voice trailed off as he stuck his head inside the vehicle. "Wow."

A third helicopter drowned out his voice.

Manny seemed to notice the helicopters for the first time. "What in the world?"

"Here." McGriffin threw him a pistol and reached inside the police car for the other shotgun. He fumbled with a box of shells and stuffed them in his pocket.

"What are you going to do?" Manny caught the shotgun McGriffin retrieved from the police car.

"Stop them." McGriffin gripped the shotgun with both hands and scanned the flight line. Two choppers were still on the taxi pad, their blades biting through the night air. McGriffin strained to see through the smoke and burning helicopters, to no avail.

Manny rolled his eyes. He turned and looked at the flight line. "I knew I should have stayed away from you fixed-wing pukes. All you do is cause me trouble."

McGriffin crouched low and sprinted for the helicopters. "Let's get going before we lose them." He zigzagged toward the closest chopper. Flames belched from the fire. He turned his head from the intense heat as he ran. He scooted in between the fire and another chopper that had not caught ablaze. In the distance the sound of fire engines grew louder, their sirens warbling as they approached. The rows of helicopters seemed to go on forever.

It was uncanny. *If whoever stole the helicopters tried to destroy the ones they left behind, then why weren't all the helicopters destroyed?* Maybe they were coming back for them, McGriffin thought, or maybe there's someone still in them.

McGriffin dropped to the ground. They'd be watching if someone was still in them. He started crawling toward the HH-53 he had just passed. He kept his shotgun in front of him, moving across the asphalt.

A roar almost knocked him flat. The fourth helicopter whirred over not thirty feet from the ground. McGriffin rolled over to his back and swung his shotgun up.

Pumping two quick blasts into the chopper, the recoil rammed into his stomach. It felt like a sledgehammer hit him. Glass crashed around him.

The chopper tilted over to the side and slipped sideways through the air. The pilot tried to straighten the listing craft, but overcorrected. The chopper rotated to the opposite side. A blade struck the ground, throwing the helicopter to the side. It ripped into a fifth helicopter that sat rotating its blades.

McGriffin scrambled backward on his heels and the back of his hands, dropping the shotgun. The two choppers burst into flames. Black smoke covered the burning. Instantly, the smoke rose and exposed the fire.

Fire engines pulled up to the first row of HH-53's. Shouts pierced the air. A gang of firemen, all dressed in silvery heat-resistant suits, strained while pulling out a series of hoses from the trucks. Soon, white foam started covering the burning helicopters.

McGriffin held up a hand to the blaze, shielding his face, wondering if there was anyone still out there. A chill swept through him as he imagined more people waiting to steal the choppers. Manny trotted up and knelt beside him.

"Great shot. Remind me to never have you on the ground when I'm airborne."

McGriffin struggled to an elbow. He looked around the rows of helicopters. No one moved except for the firemen. *Was that all of them?* He wet his lips. "How long does it take to start a chopper?"

"About two minutes, skipping checklists—one minute for the auxiliary power unit and another for the engines. You can only do that a couple of times, though, before you have to replace the whole unit."

Struggling to his feet, McGriffin grabbed Manny's arm.

"Let's go. We've got to get to Alpha Base."

"With what? Do you want to hitchhike?"

"In a helicopter!"

Manny looked incredulous. "What? It'll take more than an hour to file a flight plan, get a crew chief out here, and go through the checks."

"We don't have an hour." McGriffin waved an arm at Alpha Base in the distance. Thuds from distant explosions filled the air. "What do you think is going on out there?"

Manny wet his lips. "I was afraid you'd ask that." Manny's eyes widened. He shot a glance at the collection of helicopters still sitting on the landing pad. "What do we do?"

McGriffin started moving for the helicopters. When

Manny turned to follow, they both broke out running. McGriffin wheezed, "We'll decide when we come to it."

The firemen had just started spraying the second to last row when McGriffin and Manny arrived. McGriffin approached the choppers cautiously, just in case. . . .

Two rows back was an intact HH-53, the alert bird. Manny sprinted toward the craft. Reaching the chopper, he flung open the door and swung up into the pilot's seat. He groaned and stepped from the craft. "Shrapnel's in the control panel."

McGriffin squinted through the night. Fires bathed the pad in low light, flickering from the burning helicopters. Row after row of smoking metal; acidic smells filled McGriffin's nostrils. It looked like a blue-gray vision of hell. *Was there anybody else still out there?*

Manny's voice came from two rows down. "Over here—I've found one!"

McGriffin reached the craft. He stepped lightly on the supports and climbed aboard. Sitting, he reached for the straps as Manny quickly ran over a checklist.

"Fuel, oil pressure—jeez, I hope this thing holds together." A moment passed. "This is great. I've never flown one of these alone."

"What?!"

Manny punched at buttons. "Relax. Every rotorhead has this fantasy."

"Just a minute." McGriffin squinted at the helicopter in front of them. A lump sat underneath the fuselage. He unbuckled and scrambled down the side of their craft. He disappeared for a moment, then his head popped back into view. He held up a satchel and peered cautiously inside. "What the—it looks like plastique."

Manny jumped back in his seat and shivered. "Holy shit! Get rid of it! That's the last thing we need."

"That's a rog." McGriffin ran over to the side and gently placed the satchel down.

As McGriffin climbed on board, he said, "It looks like the explosive slipped off the bottom of the helicopter. I bet they planted them and meant to destroy every chopper they didn't take."

Manny reached for the radio and clicked the mike. "Tower, this is unscheduled HH-53 requesting permission for VFR takeoff." Waiting a scant second, he switched through the channels. "No traffic at all." He flipped a series of switches to the left of the radio and tried the microphone again. "Nope. Even the secure channels are down. At least I tried.

"Ready?" Manny glanced over at McGriffin. Without waiting for McGriffin to answer, he punched at the APU. A shrieking whine built up, winding from low bass to a high shrill. Manny intently watched the dials, counting to himself.

Just as McGriffin thought his head was going to explode from the noise, Manny pushed a succession of buttons and reached down to his right. He muttered to himself: "Number one." The left engine coughed, then started screaming. "Two." McGriffin watched Manny count to thirty. The helicopter pilot then said, "Two," and the other engine came to life. He reached to the top of the cockpit. "Release rotor blades . . . and advance engine—pull pitch: hold on!"

The HH-53 seemed to leap up into the air, leaving the concrete in a dizzy elevator ride. The ground drew away from them. Dozens of fire fighters turned their heads skyward, their faces reflecting the glow of the smoldering fires.

Manny tilted the craft toward Alpha Base.

As they approached, McGriffin strained to see what

was going on. The flashes grew brighter. Smoke and fire covered the ground. "They're under attack!" He motioned for Manny to see. "That's the barracks and command post. It looks like a bomb hit them."

Debris covered Alpha Base. Most of the searchlights were out. Burning buildings belched smoke, adding to the gloom. Overturned jeeps and trucks lay scattered throughout the complex, victims of mortars and bazooka rockets. McGriffin squinted at the bunkers burrowed in the vast crater. Every so often a dark object would sprint in between the storage units.

McGriffin pointed to a bunker near the fence. A long dark vehicle squatted just inside the crater. A gaping hole bore straight through the fence to where the vehicle sat. "Try and get a closer look. Swing around the side of that bunker."

Manny swung the helicopter around, tipping to the side. As they rounded the bunker, McGriffin spotted someone pointing a rifle up to their chopper.

"Pull back—he's going to shoot!" McGriffin pushed back in his seat. As Manny jerked the craft up, a jeep came from behind a bunker. The person on the ground swung around and shot point-blank at the vehicle. By the time the person turned back around, Manny had already pulled the helicopter up.

McGriffin drew in a breath. "Let's get some altitude."

Manny responded by increasing the rate of climb, pulling the Jolly Green well up into the night sky. An explosion on the ground rocked their craft.

"What was that?"

Manny responded by bringing the craft up faster. Alpha Base receded below them, dwindling in size until they were nearly a mile up. Manny took the craft into a slow circle, keeping Alpha Base in the center.

McGriffin took a quick inventory of their weapons:

two pistols and a shotgun. "Do you have any guns on board?"

"We're rescue choppers, remember? Not special ops. The only thing close are two flare guns in back."

McGriffin leaned forward and grabbed at the microphone.

Manny looked over to him. "What do you think we should do?"

"Notify someone."

Manny flipped through the frequencies. Nothing. "Who? With my HF out, what do you want me to do—yell? Who can we contact?"

"I don't know. Anyone. We've got to *do* something." McGriffin slouched back in his seat.

McGriffin tapped at the microphone. "Did you try Guard?" He referenced the emergency UHF radio channel.

"Yeah. No one there."

McGriffin tried for himself. After several minutes of picking up static and garbled transmissions, he slammed the mike against the console. "We must be smack in the center of null." McGriffin thought for a moment. "What's the nearest Air Force base?"

Manny kept his eyes on the instruments. "From Wendover? Probably Hill, in Ogden, Utah. Maybe Mountain Home."

"Hill's what, three hundred miles away?"

"Close enough. How's that going to help us?"

"The secure radio link—isn't the scrambled signal bounced off a satellite back to the command post?"

Manny looked puzzled. "You mean SATCOM? Sure, but we can't raise command post—you just tried."

"I know. But what's to prevent us from bouncing the secure signal off the satellite to Hill?"

Manny opened his mouth, then shut it. "It's not

172

that simple. The secure link has an encrypted data byte that directs the satellite to squirt the secure transmission back to Wendover's command post. We'd have to figure out what byte corresponds to Hill, then change the bit pattern to get a message to them."

McGriffin leaned over the data panel and studied the console. "That's what I thought. Which byte controls the destination?"

Manny pointed to a label marked DESTBYTE. "I told you, it's already preset to Wendover. You'll never figure out what Hill's pattern is."

McGriffin picked up the mike and started pressing the destbyte button. "We don't have to—once we get through to someone, they'll relay us on to Hill."

Manny nodded slowly. "I guess that's why you're the major and I'm the captain."

"You got it." McGriffin turned his attention to the radio. "Mayday, mayday. This is Wendover reporting a Broken Arrow. I say again, Wendover reporting a Broken Arrow: nuclear emergency. Can you read?"

A voice came over the radio. "Stand by one, Wendover. We copy and are ready to verify. Please transmit your verification code."

The radio went silent. McGriffin turned white. Manny frowned at him. "Go ahead. Give it to them."

McGriffin wet his lips. "I don't have it."

"What do you mean you don't have it? Command post has standard verification codes for secure transmissions—I know, I've worked there before. They change weekly. Go ahead and tell them."

"Please verify Broken Arrow, Wendover."

"I *forgot*. Chief Zolley took care of all classified traffic . . ." His voice trailed off as he realized the weakness of his excuse. McGriffin looked hopefully to Manny. "What about your codes? Can't we use the codes you fly with?"

"We pick up those codes only when we fly—besides, they change *daily.*"

"Wendover, we are breaking off your link on my count: three, two—"

"Wait, wait. This is Major William McGriffin, serial number 227–92–9116FR, commander of the Wendover command post. Alpha Base is under attack from unknown forces. They are breaking into our nuclear weapons storage bunkers."

"Wendover, we *have* to have verification. Now—"

"You don't understand! I am not at my command post. I'm in an HH-53 approximately one mile above Alpha Base. The command post was attacked during an assault on Alpha Base. We have to get some help out here."

A calmer voice came over the radio, replacing the first person they talked to. "Major McGriffin, you have sixty seconds to convince me that you're who you say you are. You'd better speed out, mister, because I'll lose my patience if you're playing games with me."

Speed out. He hadn't heard that term since he was a cadet. *Great, just what I need. Some bogie who probably thinks he's still on Wing staff.* He leaned into the mike. "Try raising Wendover—every communications channel off the base is down. Go ahead, try it."

Thirty-five seconds passed before the voice came back. "All right, so we can't raise Wendover. We're checking your background and should have a reply within the hour—"

"That's too long! They'll be gone by then!"

The voice on the other end of the secure link drew in a breath. "Then what the hell do you want me to do? Wendover's out in the middle of nowhere."

McGriffin spoke quickly. "Get a squadron of F-16's out here from Hill. It's not over half an hour away—

they could stop the helicopters from airlifting the nukes out of Alpha Base."

It sounded like an argument was taking place on the other end. Muffled voices came over the airways. The link cleared up and the voice sounded strained. "Major McGriffin, if I'm going to relay this without proper verification, I'm going to need some sort of proof you're who you say you are. We've alerted DNA and the NEST team for you—"

"I gave you my serial number. What the hell else do you want? All you have to do is check with any outfit that monitors Alpha Base."

"And I told you we're checking that out. Now convince *me.*"

McGriffin slumped back in his seat. The super Jolly Green Giant's blades made a sound that dug into his gut. Below him flames and smoke still broiled up from Alpha Base. *Wasn't there anything he could do?* He started to retort when it hit him.

Colorado cuckoo—of course, the guy's a grad! After all these years, graduating from the Blue Bastille finally helped him out. He clicked the mike excitedly. "You said something a minute ago: speed out."

The voice came back cautiously. "Maybe I did. What about it?"

"What squadron were you in?"

Silence. Then, "Three."

"Before or after it became professional?"

"What the hell are you doing—" The voice stopped, then came back slowly. "I see. All right, McGriffin. What was Three's nickname and why did they change it?"

"It *was* 'Thirsty Third,' but the comm decided drinking was unprofessional and changed it to 'Cerberus Three.'"

A full minute passed. "You've just about convinced

me, McGriffin. But that was something someone could have dug up by doing their homework. Give me one more thing that even a *touri* wouldn't know."

McGriffin racked his brains. There had to be something that he would have done, or said, or read, as a cadet that no one outside the Wing would know. . . . Turning red, he drew in a breath and started singing:

"She was a virgin in her freshman year,
　　she was a virgin with her conscience clear.
She never smoked or drank or had it yet—
　　she was the idol of her campus you can bet.
And then she met that guy from the Academy,
　　that was the end of her virginity.
She had it once and how it felt so good (felt so good),
　　she even wanted to do it again: on the Terrazzo;
　　she even wanted to do it again: with sabers and guidons;
　　she even wanted to do it again: and there was Grandma,
　　swinging on the outhouse door!"

McGriffin held his breath, embarrassed.

Manny watched him with wide eyes.

A new voice came over the secure link. "Major McGriffin, this is Hill command post. I understand you have a little problem. What can we do for you?"

18

Vikki pressed herself against the side of the bunker. Renault scrambled up the top, kicking dirt down the side in tiny rivulets. Vikki slowed her breathing. It seemed as though her gasps could be heard all over Alpha Base.

Gunfire cackled in the distance. High-pitched "pops" punctuated the air as mortars found their targets. The cool night air seemed hot now, after the incursion down into the heart of Alpha Base. Vikki fought to regain her composure. Crouching, Renault signaled for her to join him. Balancing her rifle, she toed her way up the dirt berm. She grasped a bush and pulled herself up. When she reached the top, Renault cautioned her to keep low. She edged over on her stomach.

177

Renault pointed to a group of men mulling over a radio. "The big black guy in the middle—the one with insignia on his collar. He's an officer."

"What rank?"

"Can't tell from here." Renault scooted backward. Vikki followed, and when they were hidden from sight, Renault whispered, "We've forced them to splinter into small groups. This guy just might be our baby. Wait here while I coordinate this."

Vikki only nodded. As he moved backward, Renault's face reflected the fires that dotted Alpha Base. Only twenty minutes ago they were overwhelmingly outnumbered. But Renault's surgical removal of the barracks, command post, and security post had turned the odds in their favor. Who'd have thought that Renault's fifty men would have the Air Force on the run? she thought.

Renault insisted that she and Harding split up, arguing that they had too little experience in tactical movement and they'd only hurt each other if they went together.

Renault scooted back up to her. "Here's the plan, Ms. Osborrn. I want you to move to the side, and when I signal, roll off the bunker and start shooting. *Don't* roll to the front—you'll be our diversion while two other teams jump them. So keep to the side, away from us—got it?"

Vikki nodded and grasped her rifle.

"All right." He slapped her on the shoulder. "We're waiting for your shots—get moving."

As she crawled along the top of the bunker to the side, Renault flashed hand signals. When she reached the edge, Renault pointed at her and mouthed "Now."

Vikki took two quick breaths, brought the rifle over her head, and started rolling. She let off a succession of rounds.

Shots peppered the bunker, ricocheting off the thick steel door and zinging into the dirt. Vikki kept her finger on the trigger. She held her breath, the world spinning crazily around, dirt grinding into her face.

Someone screamed. A grenade went off over her head—then the shooting stopped.

She pushed up from the ground. Rounding the bunker's corner, she saw Renault and six of his men standing over a group of security policemen. She trotted toward the group. Renault looked up as she approached. He held his rifle to the officer's head but spoke to her. "Good work."

He turned back to the officer. "One more time. How do we get into the bunkers?"

The man slowly shook his head back and forth. "Felowmate, Curtis L., First Lieutenant, United States Air Force. Serial number 765–2—"

Renault toed Felowmate. "Cut the act, Lieutenant. We both know we're not at war, and you're not a POW—the Geneva conventions don't apply here. That's why you're going to tell us how to get into these bunkers. So what is it—do you cooperate or not?"

Felowmate wet his lips. Lifting his head, he heaved out, "Felowmate, Curtis L., First Lieutenant—"

A burst of shots sent everyone sprawling. Renault knocked Vikki down. He rolled over on top of Felowmate, keeping the husky lieutenant pinned to the ground. A crash, then an explosion ejected material over the group. Smoke boiled over the adjoining bunker.

Renault sprang to his feet. "Cover the area—" He stopped and brought his rifle up as a figure stumbled into the area.

"Dr. Harding! What are you doing here?" Renault let his rifle hang. Vikki picked herself up and turned to cover the lieutenant.

Harding staggered to the front of the bunker. He placed a hand on the massive steel door and wearily dropped his rifle. "I think we tracked the last of them down. We lost only five of our men, but we must have gotten twenty of the fascists—"

"I *told* you to watch outside the fence. They could be mounting a counterattack any time now. And you lost five men doing it!"

Harding scowled. "Yeah, that's right. What about it?"

Renault set his mouth. "Those five men were ten percent of my force. And that ten percent may be all that's standing between us and the rest of the Alpha Base. The next time I order you to do something, you do it—understand?"

"No I don't. Just who the hell do you think is in charge here, Colonel? Your orders are to assist us." Harding stood toe to toe with Renault. Neither man gave in.

Renault slowly balled his hand into a fist, then released the tension. He took a step backward. "Very well, Dr. Harding. But may I *suggest* that any further incursions first be cleared by me." A faint smile tugged at his lips. "My men may become confused if they hear conflicting orders."

"Just make sure there are not any conflicting orders, Colonel," Harding spat out.

Renault twirled. He nodded to Vikki. She stood with a rifle covering Lieutenant Felowmate. He knelt beside the young lieutenant and said gently, "One more time: how do you open the bunker?"

"Felowmate, Curtis L., First Lieutenant, United States Air Force, 765–23–9901."

"All right, I've had enough." He jerked his rifle up and pointed to one of his men. "Get the youngest airman and bring him here. That one." He motioned with his head to one of the five security policemen lying facedown in the sand.

Renault's men jerked the security policeman to his feet. The man's face was flushed. He breathed rapidly; a wet stain soaked his camouflaged battle-dress uniform. They shoved him toward Renault.

Renault knelt before Lieutenant Felowmate. He spoke softly. "You've got a choice. Either get us into the bunkers or we start shooting your men. Right here, one man every minute. And if we kill everyone, we round up some more. It's your decision—you've got one minute."

Renault tapped his watch. Felowmate remained mute, staring into the ground. Vikki shuffled her weight from one foot to the other.

"Thirty seconds." Renault glanced at Felowmate. The lieutenant didn't budge.

The seconds passed. "Fifty . . . fifty-five . . . one minute. Well?" Renault looked up from his watch.

When Felowmate refused to answer, Renault searched out Harding. "Dr. Harding—would you care to do the honors?"

Harding stepped up to the young airman. Vikki took an uncertain step back. Harding whipped a pistol up to the security policeman's head. A bullet exploded, spraying fine red mist over Felowmate. Renault turned back to Lieutenant Felowmate and said, "Well?" The lieutenant stared at the ground, shaking. After no reply, Renault snapped, "Bring the next youngest."

Harding blinked, emotionless. He stood examining the pistol, running his hands over the barrel.

He's a changed man, Vikki thought. Did he still care as much about the nukes as he did about killing people? The deaths that night—first Britnell, because it was necessary; then the kids, because they *might* tell; and now these security policemen, because they had information they wouldn't divulge.

Renault's men threw the body to the side. As they brought the next security policeman forward, the airman started sobbing.

Felowmate squeezed shut his eyes, his body racked with shaking.

Again Renault knelt. "Sixty seconds . . .

"Thirty . . ."

"Fifty . . . fifty-five—"

"Stop—*stop!*" Felowmate's body grew slack. He shook his head, crying. "Please. No more. No more—they're . . . my men."

Renault straightened, his rifle pointing to the ground. "Bring the lieutenant." Vikki and Harding followed Renault to the bunker to where a metal case was embedded next to the steel door. Felowmate was shoved toward them. Renault shouldered his rifle and stepped up to the metal case.

"All right, Lieutenant. Does this contain the mechanism to open the bunker?" Felowmate nodded stiffly. "Good. That's what I thought. Open it."

Felowmate wet his lips. "I . . . can't."

"Lieutenant," said Renault wearily. "This time I'll give you no time to decide. Either open the bunker or your men will die."

"Wait—I . . . I'll open it. I'm not trying to pull anything. It's just that I *can't* do it without the keys."

"What the hell are you talking about?" Harding stepped up to the box and smashed his rifle butt into it. Another blow opened the metal door. Harding peered into the box and whirled. "There's no keying device in here! What are you trying to pull?"

Vikki stepped up. "Anthony—"

Harding stopped abruptly.

Renault raised his brows at Vikki. He directed his question to the lieutenant. "Well?"

Felowmate answered steadily, "It's a hologram. The keying mechanism uses two holograph interference devices to complete the connections necessary for opening the door—"

"Oh, shit." Harding banged his hand against the box.

"Shut up and let him finish," barked Renault.

Felowmate wet his lips. "Both holographs are in the Alpha Base command post. I can't open the bunker without them."

Renault turned and squinted in the distance. The Alpha Base command post lay in ruins at the top of the crater, a half mile away. The rest of the buildings in the complex still belched smoke. Renault took a second making up his mind.

"All right, tie up the remaining airmen—unlace their boots and use their shoelaces. When you're done, strike out for the command post—we'll be around the closest bunkers after we get the holographs from the command post. Any questions?" Looking around, Renault deferred to Harding. "Your choice, Doctor. Do you want to help tie them up, or come with us—it doesn't matter to me."

Harding slapped another cartridge into his rifle. "Let's go. I'll cover you."

Renault pushed Felowmate along after assigning one of his men to take the point. Vikki stepped alongside Renault as they started off. Keeping close to the bunkers, they tried to make it to the command post as fast as they could without actually running.

The hijacked helicopters still hovered above Alpha Base, darting in between bunkers as they ferreted out security policemen. The crafts provided tangible proof of their dominance over Alpha Base.

They traversed the half mile in six minutes. Vikki was out of breath by the time they peered at the command post from behind a bunker. The building was less than fifty yards away. No guards were visible.

Mortar shells whizzed over their heads and exploded every thirty seconds—Renault's men were still keeping the remaining security policemen away. Renault knelt, keeping a hand around Felowmate's arm.

"Ms. Osborrn, as soon as we're back, sound 'Recall' and direct the choppers to land. I'd suggest they land farther inside Alpha Base so any snipers outside the base won't have a shot. We'll be back shortly." He turned to Felowmate. "All right, Lieutenant. You had better not be pulling my leg on this."

"What's to prevent you from killing me the second you get the key?"

"Nothing—except my promise to you as another officer."

Felowmate snorted. "I wish I could believe you."

"You don't have any other choice, now, do you?" Renault shoved him forward with his weapon. "Move it, Lieutenant."

Felowmate stumbled forward, then started trotting.

As they moved toward the command post, Vikki leaned up against the bunker and looked around. Renault's men had spread throughout the bunkers, leaving her and Harding alone. Harding blinked at her and shook a cigarette from a pack. He lit it and turned away.

Vikki glanced at her watch and closed her eyes.

Forty-five minutes. After that, Renault's safety margin was up, and who knew what kind of counterattack they were going to get?

Saturday, 18 June, 2341 local

Hill AFB Gunnery Range, Utah

"Jerry—copy that?"

Captain Jerry Allison hesitated before replying. His F-16B wingman was not over half a mile behind him, flying a loose "two ship" formation. It was bad enough being pulled out of a sound sleep on a Saturday night to fly in the Wing's annual Operational Readiness Inspection. But now to be jerked from the ORI and routed to Wendover—the flight seemed a nightmare.

The bomb range lay fifty miles to the north. The F-16's were overloaded as it was: a full load of 515 rounds of 20mm ammo for the multibarreled cannon, two wing-tip mounted AIM-9J/L Sidewinders with four more on the outer underwing station, and laser-guided cluster bombs on the inner underwing station. The bird felt heavy to Jerry, but checking his fuel, the drop tanks gave them plenty of time to get to Wendover and loiter before he had to drop them.

The Wing operations officer had been cryptic in the redirection. His tone and the dropping of a secure phrase convinced Jerry that the operations officer meant business. If their National Security Agency secure radios hadn't been down for the ORI, he might have been able to get the full scoop as to what was going on. As it was, "utmost discretion"—especially from an ops officer who usually held the Wing on a tight leash—meant something *big* was up. Especially when they were told to seek out an HH-53 directing the "events." Jerry clicked his microphone and spoke in clipped sentences.

"We've been cleared to twenty-five. Let's get there —use 'utmost discretion.'"

"Question, Jerry. What's he mean?"

Jerry answered slowly. "I'm not sure. This might be part of the ORI."

"That's a rog. Hope we're not jumped by bandits from Redflag. Do those clowns know we're hot?"

"I don't think we have to worry about that." Jerry rocked his wings. "Ready to break on my count: ready, ready—now." Jerry pulled back on the stick, his arm resting on the console. Unlike the conventional hydraulically controlled aircraft, Jerry had to keep a constant four pounds of pressure on his fly-by-wire control system. The F-16's drew up to their cruising altitude of 25,000 feet before leveling off toward Wendover.

2343 local

Alpha Base

Major McGriffin leaned over and peered out the cockpit. One mile below, three stolen helicopters patrolled Alpha Base. They ducked in and out of the Pit, corralling elusive security policemen who roamed the complex. As he watched, the helicopters moved toward each other. They dipped down into the crater holding Alpha Base, kicking up dust from their descent. Men streamed toward the HH-53's, emerging from the shadows.

McGriffin started to count the terrorists, but stopped after reaching thirty. Terrorists still lobbed mortars outside Alpha Base, keeping the resistance low. Several explosives racked the narrow road leading into Alpha Base from Wendover, pitting the access road and runway with craters.

They've really covered all the bases, McGriffin thought. The few vehicles that attempted to approach Alpha Base were quickly destroyed, either from surgical strikes mounted from the patrolling helicopters or from a rain of mortars and rockets from the terrorists on the ground.

Manny kept a running commentary of the assault over the secure radio. Once McGriffin had convinced them that he was on the up and up, everybody and his brother wanted to get in on the act. They patched McGriffin to the three-star general heading up the Defense Nuclear Agency. After a short synopsis, the NEST oversaw efforts to reinforce the troops at Wendover.

Several security teams from the Department of Energy, remotely based at the Nevada Test Site, were being airlifted to Wendover. Marines from Pendleton, sitting alert with the Air Force's TransAtmospheric Vehicles at Edwards, were the closest ground troops available, but they were still over sixty minutes away.

F-111's from Mountain Home, Idaho, and everything that Nellis AFB, Nevada, could throw at them headed their way. Tankers from Beale AFB in California were launched to provide air-to-air refueling. But they all had an estimated time of arrival of over an hour. McGriffin knew it would be too late.

Manny handed the secure mike to McGriffin. "You're going to have to take over. I've got to get ready for those F-16's."

"What do you mean, get ready?"

Manny switched on an outside strobe, landing lights, and all the cabin lights. "I mean that since we have a stealth exterior, I don't want those hotshot fighter pilots running into us while they're buzzing Alpha Base."

"Oh . . ."

McGriffin turned up the volume on the secure link. Three voices were trying to talk at once. As far as McGriffin could tell, DNA, DOE, and Air Force personnel were having a pissing contest, trying to get an update on what was going on. McGriffin tried to speak into the microphone.

"Wait a minute—I can't understand anything anyone is saying—hold on. No, sir, I cannot understand you—but, I said—"

He finally switched the radio off in disgust. "I'll call them back when something changes."

"Actually, I wanted to do that—but I figured that since you're the senior officer, I'd give you the pleasure."

"Yeah, thanks." McGriffin searched the skies. "Any idea when these 16's are going to show?"

Manny consulted his watch. "We should be within radio contact anytime now. They'll be broadcasting on ultra-high frequency. Their call sign is Falcon One and Two."

"Really original." McGriffin clicked to the prearranged frequency. "This is Wendover command post calling Falcon One and Two, do you copy?"

McGriffin tried a few more times before a static-filled voice answered, "Wendover, this is Falcon One. Our ETA is five minutes. We're dropping down to altitude. Can you confirm your identity?"

"You'll have to check with Hill on that one, Falcon One."

A long moment passed; the fighters must have been conferring with their squadron on their own frequency. "Wendover, I'm supposed to ask you—what's a Loose Hog?"

Manny frowned at McGriffin. McGriffin snorted and clicked his mike. "Loose Hogs was the nickname given to Loretta Heights, an all-girls' school in Denver. Cadets dated them—"

"That's a rog, Wendover. What are your orders?"

"Stand by, Falcon One. We'll have it to you shortly." McGriffin clicked off the microphone. "All right!" McGriffin pounded Manny on the back.

The helicopter pilot smiled bleakly, keeping his hands on the stick. "Settle down. I've still got to fly this thing, you know."

McGriffin shot a glance out the cockpit. A group of terrorists gathered around one of the bunkers. "The fighters showed up just in time."

"Yeah," muttered Manny. "Knowing those clowns, they'll probably brag they saved Alpha Base all by themselves."

"At this point I couldn't care less. Here." McGriffin spread out a map and smoothed it on his knee. "Try to keep a watch on those guys down there while I try to vector our fighter friends in."

"Right."

Colonel Renault emerged from the building with Lieutenant Felowmate. Renault prodded the young black lieutenant with his rifle. Mortars still zoomed over their head as Renault's team ensured that no one was going to try to counterattack. The fires had subsided, but the air was still filled with acrid smoke.

Vikki waited until they were halfway to the bunker before contacting the helicopters on the walkie-talkie. Almost immediately the HH-53's swung from their sentry above Alpha Base and circled an opening between bunkers. As they descended, Vikki estimated the landing area was two hundred yards away. She shouldered her rifle and moved out to greet Renault.

"How did it go?"

Felowmate looked sullen as Renault shoved him forward. The colonel beamed. "Great. All we need is a bunker."

Vikki jerked her head behind her. "The choppers landed. There's plenty of bunkers over there."

"Let's move it, then." Renault took a quick look around. "Where's Dr. Harding?"

"I'm not sure—probably making sure the mission will succeed."

"I'm sure he is." Renault shoved Felowmate forward.

The path to the helicopters was dark. Every time they passed a bunker, Vikki squinted into the shadows, trying to see if anyone was hiding.

Harding met them as they approached. Ten additional security policemen lay on the ground, their hands tied over their heads and their boots all unlaced. Renault wore a thin smile. "Congratulations, Dr. Harding. If I'd known you were such an excellent stalker, I would have hired you years ago."

Harding ignored Renault's sarcasm. "Just think of them as catalyst for our young friend to open up the bunker."

Renault pushed Lieutenant Felowmate up to the helicopters. He chose the nearest bunker and directed the man to open it. As Renault waited, Harding nudged the captured security policemen in front of the bunker. Renault lit a cigarette and waved smoke away. "Lieutenant, we've wasted enough time sparring with each other. You know I promised you your life if you opened the bunker. Don't make me shoot you and your men if you fail to keep your side of the bargain, eh?" Renault drew on his smoke and watched the officer.

Felowmate set his mouth and began working. Bringing the holograph up to the box, he leaned over his shoulder and checked the bunker number: 6640. Harding shouldered his rifle and watched him. Felowmate keyed 6640 into the interference device, then waved it over the tiny glass hole. The box beeped.

Harding stepped back. "What was that?"

Renault grunted and motioned for the lieutenant to continue. When Felowmate waved the second device past the box, the bunker's steel door started to rumble. Slowly, the four-inch-thick sheet began to swing open.

"Watch out—back up," shouted Renault. The men scrambled to get out of the way. Vikki kept her rifle trained on the security policemen.

As the door crept open, Harding glanced at the prisoners Vikki watched. "Vikki, get rid of them—all they'll do is get in our way."

Vikki opened her mouth to answer when a shout erupted from a helicopter.

"Colonel—we've intercepted some radio traffic."

"What is it?"

A man ran up. "Wendover has called in reinforcements."

"How did they do that?" interrupted Harding angrily. "I thought your men were going to take care of all communications outside of the base?"

Renault ignored him. The colonel spoke patiently to the pilot. "What happened?"

"Someone is communicating with Air Force fighters. They are five minutes out and are being directed straight for Alpha Base."

"Just fucking great!" Harding spat out.

Renault persisted. "Where's the transmission coming from?"

"I'm not sure—but to transmit at that range using that frequency, they must be airborne."

Renault craned his neck and scanned the sky. The moon was just setting, and the stars blazed down in the crystal-clear night. He searched for something—"There, that bright light, directly above us."

The pilot squinted. "That's right, Colonel—it looks like a strobe!"

"And I bet it's a 53." Renault looked down. "All right, I'll take care of this." He shoved Felowmate toward Harding. "You've got it, Dr. Harding. The bunker's open, so it's your ball game."

Harding grabbed Felowmate, astounded. "What do you plan to do?"

"Misinformation. The North Vietnamese used it all the time in 'Nam—I bet the Air Force hadn't learned its lesson after all these years. By the time I'm through with these fighters, they won't know who to trust." Renault sped out toward the helicopters.

Harding looked to Vikki. His eyes were glazed, but bright. "Let's go, babe. This is what we've been waiting for." He shoved Felowmate into the bunker.

Vikki drew in a deep breath, relieved. She'd been afraid that Harding would massacre the security policemen she guarded. Now that he was gone, she motioned for Renault's men to secure the prisoners. "Make sure they won't escape."

She followed Harding and the lieutenant into the depths of the bunker. Wide yellow stripes were painted on the floor, leading into the storage facility. After a year of planning, it was all coming together.

19

The two worked in silence, Manny keeping the chopper steady while McGriffin compared the location of the terrorists with their position on the map. The temperature was steadily rising, heat diffusing into the craft from the helicopter's stealth exterior. Wiping a hand to remove the sweat from his brow, McGriffin looked up. "Ready to play Forward Air Controller?"

"Just as long as those jet jockeys stay away from us."

"That's the whole idea." Just as McGriffin reached to click his mike, a voice came over the radio.

"Falcon One, this is Wendover. There is a maverick 53 circling approximately one mile AGL over Alpha Base in violation of restricted air space. He has dropped ordnance on the Alpha Base and is dangerous. Request you ace this bandit soonest. He will

193

probably try and break into this frequency and claim he is us."

McGriffin's mouth dropped open. Manny nearly sent the helicopter into a dive. McGriffin choked. "He means us! Someone's vectoring the 16's in on us!"

He frantically tried to raise the fighters. "Falcon One, this is Wendover—that's affirmative, we're in a chopper approx one mile AGL, but this frequency is tapped. I say again, this frequency is bugged. Switch to your secure comm link ASAP."

A voice cackled back immediately. "Negatory on that, Wendover—or whoever you are. I'll need validation on you. Now what the hell is going on? Why are you flying in restricted air space? You've got one minute to clear the area. We've been unlocked from our Wing at Hill and are arming now. So *move!*"

Manny turned white. He held a steady hand keeping the helicopter at altitude. Turning to McGriffin, he wet his lips. "What do we do?"

McGriffin tried to think. Manny and he were the only two people between the terrorists and the nukes. But what could he do?

Manny raised his voice. "Come on, Bill—what do we do? I'm for lights out and getting the hell out of Dodge. What do we do?"

McGriffin shook his head and whispered, "I don't know—*I don't know!*"

2356 local

Captain Jerry Allison's F-16 broke through five thousand feet. He rocked his wings slightly by applying the barest of pressure on the fly-by-wire control. Lounging back at a thirty-degree incline, he spotted the soft glow of Wendover across the night sky fifteen miles away. He'd never been to Alpha Base—or Wendover, for that matter—but he was well aware of the drill: the thirteen-thousand-foot runway and spacious parking at Wendover could accommodate *a lot* of aircraft. He wasn't sure how many—the exact number was classified—but his Wing could fly in and strap on tactical nukes if the balloon ever went up.

Jerry flipped the Doppler onto his heads-up display. Nothing was in the air, and after a quick infrared search and track scan, he nodded to himself. He raised Pete over the radio. "IRST shows the air is clear. Whoever was up earlier must have taken our warning."

"Falcon One, this is Wendover CP. We've got an audible track on something still over Alpha Base. Request you verify and smoke him—"

"Falcon One, *this* is Wendover. I say again, you're picking up unfriendly jamming. Until you get positive confirmation, request you check out the bogies on Alpha Base—they have launched a raid on the complex and are stealing the devices stored there—"

"That's a *negative*, Falcon One. We have rescue operations currently ongoing at Alpha Base and are attempting to airlift the injured to the base hospital. Request—"

Jerry yelled over the confusion. "Pete, switch to local plus one." Jerry punched in his Wing frequency plus one band width and immediately called out, "Pete."

"Here."

"Next time they find us, switch to this minus five."

"Got it. What in the hell is going on down there?"

"Let's find out—break left and stay at altitude. I'm going in." Jerry pulled to the left and inched his stick forward. Pete remained in loose trail until Jerry started to descend; he pulled into a slow bank.

As he broke through to the low altitude, Jerry hit his speed breaks and lowered his landing gear. The F-16 grabbed at the air, slowing its air speed.

As Jerry approached Alpha Base, the devastation struck him. Buildings lay ruined, bomb craters peppered the complex. A smoky haze covered Alpha Base. He spotted a trio of helicopters squatting in the middle of a cluster of bunkers. He inched down to one hundred feet and rocked his wings. People scattered over the area started waving, raising rifles over their heads.

Jerry pulled up, bringing in his landing gear and flaps. Pete was silent until Jerry reached five thousand feet.

"What did you see?"

Jerry mulled it over. "The place was under attack."

"So where's that bandit we should smoke?"

"I'm—"

"This is Wendover—don't switch channels, I got your frequency over the secure comm link from your Wing. I say again—"

Jerry clicked his mike and interrupted the person breaking in on their frequency. "All right, *all right,* dammit. Pete—if this guy's a toad, switch to the frequency we agreed on earlier, right?"

"Button three, roger that."

Jerry turned his attention back to the voice claiming to be Wendover. He held his ship in a gentle bank over Alpha Base. "Okay, Wendover. Prove to me that you are who you say you are."

"I just spoke to Colonel Justine over the secure link and he gave me your Wing frequency—I added one band width, and here I am. But listen, those bozos on the ground are about to take off with part of Alpha Base's devices."

"Wait a minute—what devices? And where are you?"

The voice came back angrily. "You know as well as I that we can't talk about what's stored at Alpha Base—not over uncleared channels. And I'm not about to tell you where we are if you won't assure me you believe me."

Jerry hesitated; he quit speaking in clipped sentences as adrenaline rushed through his veins. "Look, how do I know you just didn't stumble on this frequency? I made a pass over Alpha Base and everything appeared to be on the up and up—"

"Open your eyes! Did you see any rescue vehicles? Ambulances? Security police cars? Make a pass over by the runway and you'll see that the access road is cratered. A flock of vehicles is trying to get across the desert to Alpha Base."

Jerry pondered the information. *Crap—why couldn't he just get the easy ones?* He wasn't even a flight commander—just a captain flying fighters, on flight pay, a beautiful wife, two kids, and no alimony . . . things were supposed to be going *great* for him. He didn't even have to think if he didn't want to—the Air Force would do that for him.

And now he had to use "utmost discretion" to save the nation?

He snorted. "Pete, jump to the new frequency. Wendover, you stay put—I'll be right back."

Jerry clicked to the Wing frequency minus five. "Pete, what do you think?"

"I don't know. You saw Alpha Base—it's your call."

"But—" He stopped. *There's no one else around, is there? Damned if I make the wrong choice.* "Pete, flip back up to Wendover." Jerry moved the radio once more. "Wendover?"

"Here."

"I'm going to make one more pass. And if you're not telling the truth, I'm hunting you down."

"Roger that."

"Hold on, Pete. Keep her steady."

"Roger that."

Jerry pulled down to Alpha Base. He clicked back to the original frequency he and Pete rode in on. "Wendover, this is Falcon One. I'm making another pass—please step out and identify yourself."

"That's a rog, Falcon One. We're waiting for your ID."

As Jerry rolled in he spotted a dozen white barrels being pushed from one of the bunkers. The barrels were shoved onto one of the helicopters. As he dipped lower, the men pushing the barrels scattered. One hauled out a pipe and pointed it at him.

"*Holy shit!* A missile!" He pulled back on the stick with his right hand, slapped the side of his fighter with his left hand to unload his decoy flares, and hit the afterburners, all in one motion. The F-16 responded sluggishly. Jerry thought fast—he was moving too slow. Dumping his ordnance, he shot straight up. As the gee indicator pegged, he cut back on the thrust. Looking back over his shoulder, half the men were scattered over the ground from his wash and load that hit the ground.

"Jerry—what's up?"

Jerry tried to keep his voice from shaking. "The bastards tried to bag me. They're loading barrels into the helicopters."

"This is Wendover CP—those are medical supplies, Falcon One. You spooked our men. They didn't know you were coming. Sorry about the misunderstanding."

"Pete, flip up to Wing plus one." A moment passed, then, "You there, Pete?"

"Yeah. What do you think about that white barrel story?"

The airborne Wendover voice broke in. "*Those,* gentlemen, are the 'devices' stored at Alpha Base. Any other questions?"

Jerry was silent. His ten-year career as an Air Force officer flashed before him. *Damn.* What if he was wrong? What if there really was a rescue operation going on down there? But he couldn't be wrong. He saw those barrels with his own eyes. And what else could they be but storage containers for nukes? He clicked the mike. "Wendover, what do you suggest?"

"Take out the helicopters."

"There are people down there—"

"You think those buildings on fire is part of a joke? A hoax? How many men do you think have died trying to prevent what is happening right now?"

Jerry bit his lip. "What about the helicopter that's being loaded?"

Silence, then: "You can't set the devices off even if you hit them—"

"What!"

"Listen—those things are *safe.* That can't detonate unless they go through a complicated prefiring sequence."

Jerry's head ached. "I don't know, Wendover. It sounds too easy. If those things go off, there's enough wallop there to take out Nevada and Utah."

"But I just told you—"

"I don't give a shit what you just told me. How do I know you're right?"

The radio was silent for a moment. "Falcon One?"

Jerry came back irritably. "Yeah?"

"How about this: you take out the two choppers that aren't carrying the devices ASAP. We'll land and try to handle the other 53 on the ground."

Jerry mused it over. "Can you handle it?"

"Probably not—but unless you've got any other ideas, we'll do it this way. And one more thing—how much fuel do you have?"

Jerry glanced at the heads-up display. His outboard tanks were nearly empty. But with his ordnance gone, he was set. "Plenty. We can loiter for another hour if we have to."

"Good." The voice from Wendover sounded grim. "Because if we don't stop that chopper, you'll have to take it out before it leaves."

"But what about the nukes!"

"Listen, Falcon One. If that chopper gets away, we might as well hang it up. How would you like a bunch of crazies holding our nation hostage?"

Jerry nodded to himself. "Pete?"

"Your call, lead. I'm glad you're in command. But that sounds damn fine to me."

Jerry nodded. He flipped the switch arming his twin-barreled cannon; it was the only armament he had left. But as a true fighter pilot, he sincerely believed that going in for the kill with a missile—standing off twenty miles and not even seeing the enemy—was for wimps. With a gun he could smoke the bastard on his own turf.

Jerry clicked his mike. "Follow me in, Wing. We're cleared hot. I'll go for the nearest 53 and you get the one at the far right."

"That's a rog, lead."

Jerry pulled into the turn, breaking out of his bank. He screamed down to attack Alpha Base.

* * *

200

Colonel Renault swore at the radio. Vikki looked up from the copilot's seat on his right.

"Do you think it will work?"

Renault tore off the headset. "I don't know."

"So what do you think we should do?"

Renault stared out the cockpit. Vikki studied his face: his jawbone worked silently, as if he were grinding his teeth. He's frustrated, she thought. And it didn't help having Harding usurp his authority.

Renault broke her train of thought. "Let's get out of here. I don't like losing contact with those fighters and that other helicopter. No telling what they cooked up."

Vikki shot a quick glance at Harding and his crew. They rolled white barrels out of the bunkers, lining them up in a queue. Only one of the helicopters had nukes in it.

"What about the rest of the nukes?"

Renault moved out of the seat. As Vikki squeezed past the seats and followed, he said, "We'll go with what we've got."

He hopped down from the chopper and strode toward Harding. Vikki stepped down and followed, jogging to catch up.

As they approached, Harding directed his crew to finish loading the helicopter. Renault's men ringed the helicopter, weapons at ready. Thirty gleaming white barrels stood lined up in a row, waiting to be loaded on the HH-53. Two men struggled with each barrel. In the corner Lieutenant Felowmate sat with his head hanging, his hands tied to his feet. Renault stepped up to Harding and spoke in a low voice.

"We've got to get out of here."

Harding frowned. "We've barely got one helicopter loaded." He pivoted and waved the men to step up the pace. Turning back, he said, "We need another ten minutes."

"If we don't leave now, there's a chance we'll never get out of here. I think that renegade chopper is vectoring those fighters in on us."

Harding stopped. "You *think*? Didn't you hear them?"

"No, but those fighters quizzed me, and I didn't like their questions."

Harding dismissed him. "Then keep watch until you know for sure."

Renault narrowed his eyes. "Look, Dr. Harding. We don't have time. If we take off now, we'll have our nukes. There's no way we'll be able to get out of here if we hesitate—"

The helicopter behind Vikki burst into flames. The explosion knocked her to the ground. Waves of heat washed over her as a second helicopter exploded. Her ears pounded. Bullets erupted around her. Renault pushed up from the ground and started yelling to his men.

"Get on the remaining chopper—*now!*"

Vikki felt a hand around her waist; her hair had come undone and now flew into her eyes. Looking up through her hair, she saw Harding swim in and out of focus. She nodded dully and struggled up. Harding helped her.

As they staggered forward, the sound of a helicopter pierced the air. On the other side of the bunker an HH-53 dipped to the ground and landed, not fifty yards away.

20

Alpha Base

Manny brought the 53 down in a combat landing: descend as fast as possible and pull up at the last moment, just before hitting the ground. McGriffin directed him away from the burning choppers—he didn't want to land too close to the terrorists.

They approached the bunkers at a dizzy rate, going down into the crater. Smoke and dust covered them, masking the last part of the descent. The bunkers were spaced fifty yards apart in a staggered pattern; they bore for a spot between three bunkers. As they approached the ground, they dipped below the top of the bunkers, hiding them from sight.

As McGriffin opened the door, the super Jolly Green Giant greased onto the ground. The bunkers rose at least a good five feet higher than the top of the helicopter. McGriffin grasped the walkie-talkie, pistol, and shotgun, waving off Manny's offer of the flare gun. "I can't carry anything else. If you lose contact with me, let's rendezvous just south of here, two bunkers away."

"Rog."

McGriffin leaped out onto the dirt just as the helicopter roared upward. It took him a few seconds to get his bearings. Spotting the burning choppers out of the corner of his eye, he ducked and ran diagonally across the clearing. He was one bunker away from the brouhaha.

He scrambled up the side of the dirt bunker. Kicking away sand and rocks, he climbed up the sloping embankment, hugging the side and keeping in the dark. He was ten feet from the top when he decided to stop. The terrorists should be just on the other side of the bunker, and were probably waiting for him.

He moved sideways, carefully trying not to disturb the fragile balance of rock and sand. Shouting and a rain of gunfire belched below him. They were literally shooting in the dark; most of the spotlights on the bunkers had been shot out. He scrunched up close to the dirt. Hanging there, he felt like a fly clinging for his life.

The men moved on. McGriffin moved cautiously sideways. Slipping once on a false toehold, he pulled himself back up to the military crest. Manny's chopper had disappeared, shooting up into the night sky where he waited for McGriffin's call.

He reached the bunker's edge. Holding on to a clump of cactus, McGriffin took a cautious peek around the corner. Six men ringed the remaining helicopter. Weapons drawn, they crouched with their backs to each other, silently guarding the surviving

HH-53. McGriffin counted seven of the white nuclear weapons storage containers. Squinting, he spotted more barrels inside the craft. He couldn't tell how many were on board, but there seemed not to be more than fifteen total.

Two men gestured at each other, standing between the seven barrels and the helicopter. Another ten men stood tensely around, their weapons pointing in the air.

McGriffin pulled back and breathed deeply. Eighteen men, he thought. He'd have to forget taking the chopper by force. But what could he do? Armed with a shotgun and pistol, he'd be lucky to get five of the terrorists before being shredded to pieces. Even radio contact with Manny wouldn't help him.

He *had* brought down one chopper earlier tonight, but that was blind luck. Besides, the 53 hadn't been more than twenty feet above him. No chance of getting that close again. McGriffin breathed a prayer.

It started to look like the only other option would be to have Falcon One come in and blow the remaining helicopter away; but how could he convince them the nukes wouldn't detonate?

If only the nuclear weapons weren't on board! It would be a piece of cake.

McGriffin started moving away from the edge when the gunfire rang out. Scrambling back for a quick look, his heart stopped: one of the terrorists held a hostage in front of him, threatening a man with a pistol. The hostage slumped forward in the man's arms. Her long blond hair drooped nearly to her waist.

Vikki Osborrn was in the middle of the confrontation.

Vikki . . . *here!*

McGriffin lurched back. He tried to slow his breathing. He felt giddy, lightheaded. He knew he was hyperventilating, but the sight of Vikki almost floored him.

With shaking hands he pulled out the walkie-talkie and spoke in a low, desperate voice. He made sure Manny understood the instructions perfectly before he started away: no matter what happened, *the fighters had to make sure that chopper didn't leave the ground!* Even if it put his own life in danger.

Feeling sick to his stomach, he crawled back across the bunker to where he could slip to a clearing, away from where the fighters would be attacking. From there, Manny would pick him up . . . after the fireworks.

Vikki tried to lay limp in Harding's arms. The dead weight should set him off balance, and more importantly, he might ignore her if the shooting started again. As Harding dragged her back to the helicopter, the physicist sparred with Renault.

"It's as simple as that, Colonel. One helicopter cannot carry all the nuclear weapons and the rest of your men. Some of them must remain until the helicopter can return."

Renault took a step toward the helicopter but backed down as Harding shook his pistol at him. "My men will not allow the helicopter to leave without them."

"They will if you order them, Colonel. I've seen your men in action. They will do whatever you tell them."

Renault swept an arm at his men. The crew surrounding the helicopter scanned the night sky. They dragged a fiber-optic guided missile, captured from the security policemen. One of the men held the launcher on his shoulder.

"You're right, Doctor. But my men are not stupid,

either. Why do you think they follow me? If they were complacent, they would not be here. They will obey me—but they will also survive." Renault took a step forward. "How many of those weapons do you need, anyway? Are you going to be able to dismantle the safeguards on all of them?"

Harding stepped backward. He reached the door of the chopper. Feeling his way with his elbow, he stepped inside. He trained his pistol on Renault the entire time. "Order your men to back off."

"I refuse to—"

"Incoming!" Renault's men sprawled to the ground in an automatic reflex. A whine escalated to a white roar as bullets peppered the ground. Renault dove toward the helicopter; Harding fell inside. Glass crashed on Vikki. She scrambled to her knees, her vision blurred by dripping blood.

Eight men fell dead to the ground, caught in the fighter's rain of hot metal. A few tried crawling to safety, but those who came to help them were mowed down. The hail of bullets marched across the clearing.

The men with the missile held their ground. Following the fighter's progress, they ignored the spray of bullets and tracked the jet in their infrared sights. Just as the fighter started to pull up, they lit the missile's tail.

Spurting flames ten yards long, the missile raced out of the bore. Hundreds of feet of fiber-optic wire spooled out, clicking against the armature. Guiding the missile in, it took less than two seconds for the device to intersect the fighter. The missile detonated.

The fighter veered off, belching black smoke. Seconds later a thundering roar filled the sky.

Vikki pushed herself into a corner. She covered her head with her hands and tried to make herself small.

Harding dragged himself over to the pilot; no one

else was on board. Helenmotz still grasped the stick, frozen in his seat. Harding held a pistol to his head. "Take off."

"I . . . can't . . ."

Harding pulled the trigger back. "I said, take off. You've got five seconds to get this bird off the ground or I'm putting a bullet through your head. One, two, three—"

"Wait, dammit." Renault stumbled on board. "We got the jet. We can still get the rest of the men on board—"

Harding coolly whipped around and pumped two shots into him. The colonel slumped forward, falling just inside the helicopter. Vikki ducked and closed her eyes. Things were happening too fast.

Turning back to Helenmotz, Harding clicked the trigger again and said, "I've got four shots and you've got two seconds. One—"

Helenmotz punched at the auxiliary power unit. Dust kicked up from the chopper's blades accompanied the high-pitched whining. The sound came from a Dantean symphony: with the front windshield gone, glass, wind, and a cacophony of noise crashed inside the helicopter. The chopper lifted only inches off the ground, then slowly rotated around.

Two of Renault's men scrambled to get on the helicopter. Harding spent three bullets killing them; they fell out the door to the ground. Harding turned back to Helenmotz.

"Get out of here!" Harding yelled over the wind.

"Only one engine is up!"

"Now!" Harding put the gun to pilot's head.

Helenmotz strained with the controls. The other engine ran up; Helenmotz pulled up on the collective to get altitude, then pushed forward on the stick. Gritty sand whipped through the helicopter.

Across from Vikki the ground twirled crazily through the open cargo door. The helicopter tipped, and she felt she would slide out. Shots tore up from below them, piercing the deck and ricocheting inside the cabin. The white storage barrels knocked against each other, straining against hastily lashed ropes. As the chopper rose higher in the air, the shots stopped.

Vikki struggled up. In the cockpit Harding grasped the right seat and stood with his legs bent, ready to cushion any jolt. He rested his pistol on the crook of his arm. Vikki steadied herself and walked uncertainly across the deck. Blood caking on her face blurred her vision.

Harding caught her out of the corner of his eye. He cracked a grin. "Half an hour and we're home free." He jerked his head at the nine white barrels lashed together in the rear of the craft. "We've done it. Each one of those babies will pull down at least a million. Pick any place you want to live, Vikki—anywhere in the world, and it's yours."

They left the glow from Alpha Base behind them. As they headed for the mountains, Vikki couldn't help feeling that the original purpose for the raid had slipped away as well.

21

E&E: Escape and Evasion. All USAF Academy cadets go through a grueling three-week survival course after their freshman year, learning E&E.

It was a skill you never forgot.

McGriffin E&E'ed through the bunkers, running in a crouch, fanning his weapon around. He ran silently, moving quickly from shadow to shadow in a random fashion, never staying in one place for too long. Every few seconds he scanned the bunkers jutting up around him and tried to pick out movement, any hint that a sniper might be targeting him.

Once he E&E'ed around another bunker, he would be at the rendezvous point, south of where he had been dropped off. He ran up the crater, and although the slope was not steep, it still drained him of energy.

He almost threw his shotgun down—the weapon

seemed heavier with every step he took. As he moved farther away from the terrorists, he grew more reckless in the E&E tactics. Soon he was running pell-mell out in the open.

Falcon One screamed overhead. Moments later the sickening explosion from the F-16's demise turned his stomach. The sound of the stolen helicopter leaving made him vomit. He had to stop and puke out his guts as the HH-53 rose over the bunker and into the night.

How many deaths would he be responsible for? The nukes on board would certainly be used against American lives.

Stumbling into a clearing, he whirled to check his position. He couldn't tell for certain, but it looked like the rendezvous area. He fumbled with his walkie-talkie. He drew in a breath and said weakly, "Manny."

"Be there shortly."

McGriffin pressed against a bunker. The stars burned serenely down, punching through the haze that permeated Alpha Base. The acrid smell was almost gone, but in its place rose something more macabre: burning flesh. McGriffin shivered, thinking about how many had died that night.

Manny's 53 bore straight down on him. It was one thing to be on board during a combat landing; standing by the landing zone was another thing entirely. The chopper fell out of the sky—with its landing lights off, it appeared as a dark blob, blocking out the stars. Just when he felt the wind from the blades, the helicopter lighted on the dirt.

McGriffin ducked and sprinted toward the craft. He swung a leg up and pulled himself on board. Manny gave him a quick thumbs-up before taking off. McGriffin pushed forward. The red cabin lights glowed dimly, outlining the instruments. He settled down in the right-hand seat and waited until Manny gained altitude before speaking.

"The F-16 didn't stop them."

"I saw. At least he punched out."

"Thank God for that. But what about the chopper?"

Manny was silent for a moment. "Your guess is as good as mine. I'm still in contact with Falcon Two—he lost him too."

"What? How could he let the chopper slip away!"

"Conductive plastics, remember? The other 53 has a stealth coating just like us, so he's virtually invisible."

McGriffin mulled it over. "How about an update from the secure link? Have DNA and the other agencies stopped squabbling yet?"

Manny glanced at the inboard digital clock. He worked his mouth wordlessly. "Another half hour and the DOE boys should arrive from the Nevada Test Site. That's about the time the rest of the fighters should start getting here. A satellite IR and radar search has started, concentrating on all possible landing sites."

McGriffin snorted. "Probably means they don't know what the hell is going on. Anything else?"

"You're still the on-site commander. Until they restore communications, and they're able to get Colonel DeVries or someone else out here, you're the senior ranking officer. The civil engineers are out patching the runway and access road—they should have it pretty well fixed up for the incoming crews. There should be enough security policemen to make a sweep of Alpha Base in the same time frame."

"Crap." McGriffin struck the console with a fist. "Still, what's taking security so long to get there? I thought Alpha Base was supposed to be nearly invincible?"

Manny was silent for a moment before answering. "I'm not a spokesperson or anything like that, Bill—"

McGriffin looked quickly up. He felt suddenly bad yelling at Manny; especially when the chopper pilot was the only sympathetic guy around for miles. "Sorry. I didn't mean to take it out on you."

"S'all right. It's just that I can't really blame them. They did have half their force out there on Alpha Base, and with the other half in the dorms, you'd think with all communications out, there'd be some screw-ups. Hell, we're lucky we were around."

McGriffin settled back in his seat. "Right. But to think we can't even find that helicopter. By the time DOE gets here, no telling where they'll be." He looked out the cockpit. They flew a mile above ground level, making a slow sweep of Alpha Base. Below them everything seemed serene. The fires flickered low. Even the smoke cleared, bathing Alpha Base in a pastoral light. If it weren't for who-knows-how-many nukes were missing, the setting would have been placid.

The idyllic sense of well-being lulled his memories back. *Vikki—what did she have to do with it? Was she kidnapped, or what? She couldn't have anything to do with it.* Or could she?

McGriffin frowned. Something tugged at his mind. What if she was part of all this? Who else to befriend than one of the Wendover command post commanders? What better way to ensure that the terrorists got all the information they needed?

But she *couldn't* have been set up to meet him—no one knew where he was going that day they met, not even himself. And she didn't get any information from him at all. He didn't even suspect; all those times he was with her.

But yet . . .

And then it hit him.

"Manny, how's your fuel?"

"Uh, pretty good. No need to worry—with just two of us, we can stay up here another few hours, although I'm not used to flying this high."

McGriffin set his jaw. "I have a hunch where those terrorists might have gone."

"Say the word."

"Head northwest for the mountains. There's a clearing where they just might be able to resupply from."

Manny looked puzzled. "The mountains? That's the last place they'll try. If you're thinking of someone flying in there to get them out, the desert has a lot more flat spots to use as landing areas."

"I know. And that's why I hope I'm wrong."

Manny stared at him for a moment before shrugging. "If you say so." He swung the craft from its pattern and started climbing; the mountains hit ten thousand feet, and he wanted to make sure the search didn't ruin their day.

Harding kept his pistol trained on Helenmotz the entire flight. The HH-53 pushed to make it over the mountains, straining to fly in the thin air. In the back, Vikki perspired from the heat and watched. Even with the cargo door open the stealth composite on the helicopter's exterior made the inside of the chopper feel like an oven.

She studied Harding during the bumpy trip. Wind careening off the rugged peaks shot up and caught them in turbulence, bouncing the craft in random jolts. Harding's face glowed red, reflecting the dials from the control console. He was a different man from when they first started. Possessed—caught up in the rush of control.

It seemed the idealism had died. And from his remarks once they took off from Alpha Base, a craving for power had replaced the enthusiastic elan to save the world. Power and money. She turned her head away. At least their main goal would be accomplished: showing the world how easy it is to steal these weapons of mass destruction.

The pilot turned his head to Harding. "We're approaching the rendezvous site."

"Take her in." Harding brandished his pistol. Helenmotz's eyes widened as Harding spoke. "Don't try anything funny—no quick movements, nothing. Just land the helicopter. Understand?"

Helenmotz stiffly nodded yes.

Soon the chopper stopped its forward motion. Helenmotz reached for the microphone. Harding shook his head. "Radio silence. You don't want them to find us, do you?" Helenmotz dropped his hand.

When they finally bounced at landing, Helenmotz looked to Harding. Harding smiled. Putting down the pistol, he said, "Secure the chopper. Good work."

Helenmotz looked relieved. He turned to power down the craft's instruments. As he swiveled, Harding whipped up his pistol and fired the silencer point-blank into Helenmotz's skull. Blood splattered over the console.

Reloading, Harding quickly pumped another round into Helenmotz's shoulder. Harding rubbed some of the warm blood on his chest, making it appear as if he were injured too. He started dragging Helenmotz out of the seat. Looking around, he spotted Vikki.

"Help me before they get to the door."

Vikki struggled upright, shocked. In a daze she stepped over Renault's body and took one of Helenmotz's arms. Grunting, they swung the dead pilot out of the seat and piled him next to Renault.

Just as they finished, a head poked through the still open cargo door.

Harding motioned to the white barrels in the rear. He feigned pain. "Hurry—unload the weapons and get them aboard the aircraft."

The man pulled himself up and widened his eyes at the bodies. Vikki recognized him as one of Renault's South American recruits. He knelt beside Renault and whispered. "Colonel?"

"Renault is dead. We barely made it out . . . everybody else died. Now quickly, before we're followed."

The man crossed himself and stuck his head out the cargo door. He yelled in Spanish, and instantly three men appeared at the chopper door.

Harding spoke to the one in charge. "The girl and I will take care of the bodies." The man grunted, and with the help of the other three started rolling the nuclear weapons out of the helicopter.

Harding and Vikki dragged the bodies out of the craft. Moving away from the C-130, they deposited them in the brush. Harding wiped his hands when they were finished. "Once we're airborne they'll never get the whole story. Fifteen minutes to load, and we're heading for Baja."

"What about Renault, Anthony? Don't you think it's a little suspicious he didn't return—and we're the only ones on the raid that did?"

Harding looked cold. "Just be thankful that you came back. I'm starting to wonder if it's a good thing or not." He turned for the C-130. Vikki drew in a breath and started after him.

22

Humboldt National Forest

Manny tore off his headset. "Have you spotted it yet?" For the past fifteen minutes he had been in communication over the secure link, speaking in a low voice so as not to disturb McGriffin.

McGriffin waited a full minute before answering. Two hundred feet below, jagged mountain peaks scraped the sky. Only the summits were visible in the scant starlight. Every so often a glint of light bore through the clouds and reflected off water in the valleys. Switching to the ANVIS-6 night-vision goggles, McGriffin strained, but still could not make out any sign of the helicopter.

He flipped up the goggles, rubbed his eyes, and looked to Manny. "Are you sure you corrected for wind?"

217

Manny nodded to the Inertial Navigation System readout. Calibrated by a laser gyro, the Inertial Navigation System was accurate to within the gravitational uncertainties of the earth. Manny retorted, "I could fly us to within a *foot* of where we took off from. If your directions are accurate, we should be right on top of that clearing."

"Sorry. Any other ideas? I *know* these coordinates are correct."

"I'll get you some more altitude. We can cover more area that way." He shot a glance at the altimeter. "It'll be touch and go, though. We're already pushing this baby's ceiling—I don't want to go too much higher."

McGriffin decided instantly. "Let's do it." He'd already made up his mind that any danger to themselves came second to recovering the nukes. If the terrorists were down there, the night-vision goggles would give them away—unless they were inside the stealth helicopter, but that was a chance he would have to take.

Manny pushed the chopper up, grabbing for altitude. The craft strained in the thin air. Slowly they crept higher, bringing more of the ground into sight. As they rose, McGriffin flipped down the goggles and scanned the ground, methodically moving from north to south.

He was almost ready to have Manny move farther west when a smear of light broke across his sight. "Wait. Bring us back to the east."

"Did you see anything?"

"I'm not sure. We're a little high to tell for sure. It might have been a deer—hold it." He held up a hand. "That's it."

"That's what?"

McGriffin adjusted the night-vision goggles by changing the diopter, then refocused the low intensity picture. "There's someone walking . . . make that four, no five, people. They're moving toward something bright. I don't have a positive on it, but I bet that's an engine mounting I see." He flipped up the infrared light amplifier. "How is Falcon Two doing?"

"He was loitering at twenty thousand, but he was sucking on fumes so he headed back. He had only enough fuel to get him back to Wendover."

McGriffin unstrapped from the copilot's seat and squeezed behind the seats. He surveyed his weapons: two pistols and a shotgun. Except for the flare guns— which were worthless anyway—things hadn't changed. Great, I'm going to save the world, he thought, and don't even have enough weapons to finish the job. Dear Lord, don't let me screw up now.

Grunting, McGriffin pushed open the cargo door, jerking when it momentarily caught. A gale of wind whooshed through the helicopter. Lying on the deck, he flipped on the goggles and peered down.

The bodies moved in a slow line, hunched over, straining with something on the ground. They moved steadily in a group as if they were rolling something— the nukes?—then rushed back to where the helicopter lay and started all over again. McGriffin couldn't make out the object they rolled the nukes to. He raised the gain and squinted.

A dark object slowly appeared in the screen, barely contrasting against the ground. *A plane!* The ground was slightly cooler than the aircraft, causing the ghostly infrared image to waver in the nightscope.

McGriffin refocused to infinity. Suddenly the bodies stood out in fine detail. One of them raised a hand and pointed upward, directly at the chopper. *They heard us. Our blades must be giving us away.* He straightened and slammed shut the cargo door. The wind died immediately.

He stepped up to the cockpit. "Manny, any more word?" Manny shook his head, his lips held tight. McGriffin took a last look down. "There's a plane down there—they're loading up the nukes, and worse, they've spotted us. They're breaking out rifles or something. We've got to stop them."

"Right. With what? Our bare hands?"

"If we have to." McGriffin grasped the back of the seat. "Look, we've got to stall them—stop them from taking off until one of the other flights of fighters gets here. Get an ETA over the secure link."

A moment later Manny lifted his head. "Twenty more minutes—but they've got our coordinates."

McGriffin drew in a breath. "That's not good enough. The plane will be gone by then."

"So what do we do?"

McGriffin looked around the helicopter. The shotgun and pistol had to count for something. "Let me down. Land me by the edge of the clearing. I'll try to sneak around and slow them from loading their plane—anything to stop them from taking off."

"Land *there*? They'll take out us out!"

"Got any other suggestions?"

A moment passed. Manny said slowly, "You're crazy. You know that? Absolutely crazy. If this was special ops, I'd lay you down over the ridge. But with the time constraint . . ." He bit his lip. "Okay, but what about me?"

"Get some altitude. I'll need you to vector the fighters in—they've got to take out that plane."

"If they hit one of the nukes, it'll take the mountain down."

McGriffin shook his head. "It's nearly impossible to set those things off. The worse that could happen is that the high explosives would detonate."

"High explosives—you mean H.E.?"

McGriffin set his mouth. "Yeah. The H.E. is used to initiate the nuclear implosion, or something like that." He wished he'd paid more attention to Lieutenant Felowmate's explanation. He turned for the rear of the craft. "Keep in contact over the link. Once I'm down, grab some air."

Manny shook his head. "Right."

Manny's combat landing number three: the other two were a piece of cake compared to this.

McGriffin lost all depth perception. They fell into the black abyss as quickly as they could. The peaks flashed by, their features painted silver by the starlight. McGriffin prayed that Manny's night vision was better than his. He didn't see the ground when they landed.

Manny screamed at him. "Out, mo-fro. Call me when you're done."

The chopper thundered upward. McGriffin rolled away from the landing area, certain that they would start shelling him. As the helicopter accelerated upward, a missile raced over his head.

Manny's helicopter lit up in the night. A doubled explosion sent the chopper rolling to the right. Light flashed inside the craft. Slowly, the super Jolly Green Giant crumpled to the ground, spinning as the blades careened off the meadow. The helicopter crashed not fifty yards away.

McGriffin watched, horrified. He got up and started running toward the downed chopper. Flames licked at the craft. He expected the helicopter to explode any moment—and at fifty yards, take him with it.

He stopped in mid-stride, suddenly throwing himself to the ground. Silence. *Were they waiting for him?*

If he tried to rescue Manny, he'd be an easy target. So what would it be—Manny or the terrorists? He couldn't get to both.

He grit his teeth. *God, help me!* A scream came from the helicopter. Manny shrieked in pain.

McGriffin tried to get his wits about him. Scanning the clearing, he quickly got his bearings. The light from Manny's helicopter splashed throughout the meadow. Behind him the plane showed up as a dark, menacing outline against the mountain. Purple flowers pocketed the field. The tall grass hid him from view. But they would be watching.

Or would they? Did they know that he got out, or did they think the chopper was coming in for a landing? Either way, he couldn't tip his hand. He backed up on his belly, trying to slide away from the helicopter and the light of its fire. Cradling the shotgun in his arms, he moved quietly back.

He tried keeping track of the distance as he drew away. Push, slide, and keep the head down—it seemed to go on forever. By the time he got to the one hundredth slide, he was out of the brightest circle of light. *Manny!*

The chopper still hadn't exploded. Maybe they had been low on fuel . . . or maybe they were just plain lucky. Manny's shrieks died to moans, now barely audible. McGriffin felt sick to his stomach.

McGriffin swiveled around and surveyed the meadow. Now that his eyes adjusted to the dim light, the plane stood out against the mountains at the end of the meadow, a good quarter mile away. *It was a C-130!* McGriffin held back a whistle of surprise. It started to come together—this was the bird from "Peterson Field" that had started tonight's nightmare.

Turning on his buttocks, McGriffin spotted the hijacked 53. Its seven blades drooping in the starlight, the chopper sat a hundred yards from the C-130. No one was around. Six white barrels dotted the field, laying in between the helicopter and plane. An unnatural stillness permeated the air. McGriffin rocked back and waited. Another moan from Manny pierced the night—

A whistle alerted him. Slowly, a figure appeared from the C-130. It rushed to one of the white barrels. Two other figures picked themselves up from beside the barrel. An expletive. Then, "Hurry up—no telling when the next one will come."

One of the figures kneeled. Grunting, he picked up a long tube. "What about the Stinger, Dr. Harding?"

"Keep it with you, you idiot—you'll get just as much warning on the next attack."

Two more figures emerged from hiding.

Then a voice that floored him. "Do you think that was the helicopter hovering above Alpha Base?" *Vikki!* "There's someone still alive on board."

"I don't know. It doesn't matter anyway. After the nukes are on board, we're leaving. So shut up and help."

McGriffin strained to see through the darkness. The figures appeared as blobs. He was closer to the helicopter than the 130, but was still at least fifty yards away. *Vikki.* It still seemed incredible—and the hardest thing to accept was that she was a *part* of all this. From the tone of her voice, she obviously wasn't a prisoner. It cut through him like a knife: she was of the terrorists.

Through the disbelief, the reason why he was there reared its head: he had to stop the C-130.

Vikki's voice shook him again. "Listen, Anthony—I don't give a shit about putting any more of these nukes on board. You've got five already—how many more are you going to need?"

One of the figures strode up and grabbed her arm. It was the one they called Dr. Harding. "I said, get to work. Every one of those containers is another million in the bank. Ten more minutes, that's all it'll take."

She shook off his arm. "And I'm not leaving another maimed body—for someone who's fighting for peace, you sure as hell have killed your quota tonight. I'm pulling that guy out of the fire." She stomped away.

"Yeah, and don't forget about how you pumped poor innocent Britnell with lead, you bitch. What else are you going to do now? Screw that helicopter pilot after you save him?" He threw a rifle after her. It bounced on the ground and disappeared in the tall grass. "We're leaving in ten minutes, with or without you."

Vikki suddenly turned. She rummaged through the grass and found the rifle that had been thrown at her. Glaring, she stalked wordlessly away, toward Manny's helicopter. Harding turned to the others and barked out an order. "Hurry—get these on board." He pointed to one of the men. "Rev up the engines." Throwing a glance over his shoulder at Vikki, he turned and put a shoulder to one of the barrels. He scowled, "Ten minutes and we're out of here."

He had a plan.

McGriffin waited as Vikki tromped past. She swept twenty feet from him. As her legs brushed through the grass, McGriffin crouched and followed her. He kept near enough so that his rustling would not stir the other terrorist's suspicions, yet kept far enough away so that she couldn't hear him.

As he followed, his back started to hurt. He tried to keep low in the foliage, but even the two-foot height of the grass couldn't hide him entirely.

Vikki reached the helicopter. Placing her rifle in a

bare spot, she glanced over her shoulder to the C-130. When she turned toward him, McGriffin hit the dirt and let out a muffled "ooof." Sweat formed on his brow.

Vikki stepped to the burning chopper. She reached up and touched a metal piece that hung at a crazy angle to the ground. Stepping lightly up, she pulled herself onto the 53. Smoke rose around the craft's periphery. An acrid odor of JP-4 and burnt plastic permeated the air. Manny's moans had died to whimpers.

As Vikki poked around, McGriffin sat sweating, debating how to approach her.

She was his only ally—his only possible way to stop them. Without the helicopter to vector the fighters in, it was hopeless. But yet . . . if she was one of them, could he convince her to help him?

And if pigs had wings, they could fly.

Reality hit him smack in the face: he was kidding himself, molding her into what he wanted her to be. Vikki might be showing some soft side of her personality, but if she was *really* in on this raid—and if she'd really killed a man, as Harding had just said—he wouldn't be able to change her mind. At least not in the next five minutes.

He inched away from the helicopter. His plan dissolved before his eyes. Quickly turning, he started to make his way back to the C-130. Back to where he might be able to do something to the plane—the fuel tanks, anything. If he had to, he could always pump a few rounds in the instruments and wing tanks in a suicide stand.

A trigger clicked behind his head. "Make another move and you're dead." McGriffin froze in his tracks. "Drop it." His shotgun fell to the ground. He stood, raising his hands over his head, not offering any resistance. "Turn around." As he slowly turned, Vikki came into view.

Her eyes widened. Her rifle dropped momentarily, then straightened as she tightened her grip. Her eyes drew together and flashed as if she were betrayed.

They stared at each other. Behind her the helicopter belched smoke, setting her body in a surrealistic frame. She whispered, "Well?"

McGriffin drew in deep breaths. His trembling abated. He kept silent.

Her rifle wavered. "Bill, what . . . do you know what you're doing? How did you get here?"

McGriffin blinked and jerked his head toward the downed helicopter. "Vikki . . ."

She seemed to notice his uniform for the first time. She raised her voice and tightened her grip on the barrel. "How *dare* you. You didn't tell me you were one of *them*." She spat out the word.

"Vikki . . ." He shook his head. "You don't know what you're doing—"

McGriffin stopped at a rustling behind him. Harding's voice broke through the night.

"Well, well. It looks like old home week here. Who is this, Vikki? Another one of your GI Joes you've been screwing on the side? Dragged him out of the helicopter for a little action, huh?"

Vikki held her rifle steady on McGriffin. "Don't be an ass, Anthony. I didn't drag him from anywhere. He was trying to get to the plane. Lucky I caught him, too."

As Harding walked into view, McGriffin's heart sank. *Looks like I've tied one up big time. Anything else from here on out would only be a plus.* An instance at the Academy roared through his mind. It was unarmed combat, and the instructor was telling them about impossible situations: *never* give up; *never* allow yourself to be shot between the eyes. Better to go down swinging and have half a chance than placidly have your hands tied behind your back and be executed.

Harding broke his chain of thought. "So where do you know this teddy from?"

Vikki hesitated. "He's one of the fascists I met."

"An officer?" Harding dropped his jaw in mock amazement. He brought his pistol up and brushed off McGriffin's shoulder boards. "Too bad you couldn't have nailed one of the really big ones. I hear that intelligence is inversely proportional to rank: the higher they come, the dumber they are. And compared to your friend Britnell, this bozo must really be an idiot."

He jerked his head back to Vikki. "We're loaded. Kill him. We're ready to go." He started toward the C-130.

Vikki stared at McGriffin.

After ten steps Harding stopped and said irritably, "I *said*, kill him. If he's just a fascist, what's the problem?" He narrowed his eyes and studied Vikki.

Harding was just at the edge of McGriffin's peripheral vision. Vikki watched McGriffin. Her eyes grew round.

McGriffin whispered, *"Vikki!"* and took a step forward.

Harding whipped up his pistol.

McGriffin primed himself. *I'm not going to stand here and be shot!* He drew in a deep breath. Adrenaline raced through his veins. Vikki's rifle wavered. He flexed his legs and started to jump—

"Shoot him *now*, dammit!"

Vikki trembled.

Harding swung his pistol to Vikki and pulled off a shot. Vikki collapsed as McGriffin dove into the brush.

McGriffin rolled, keeping his head tucked to his chest. Burrs and twigs tore into his skin. Pollen, shaken loose from his rolling, drove into his nostrils. He sneezed.

He opened his eyes, still rolling. Shots peppered the ground. *Two, three, four*—a red-hot needle tore into his arm. It felt as if his shoulder would fall off. He grabbed at the wound and crouched lower.

Scrambling, he ran a crooked path away from the shots. Harding crashed after him, emptying the pistol. A volley of shots rang out, but they zinged by, missing him. Reaching the edge of the meadow, McGriffin dove into the thick brush. Crawling on his hands and knees, he fell to the ground. He tried to catch his breath, then slowed his breathing so it wouldn't give him away.

Pressing his wound with his hand, he gritted his teeth at the pain. He balled his body up and tried to make himself invisible by pushing his head to the ground.

Feet thrashed in the brush. The search continued briefly, a mixture of bullets and cursing filling the air. Finally, Harding yelled out in disgust, "Let's *go*, dammit. He can't stop us now."

Waiting until the footsteps receded, McGriffin raised his head and peered toward the meadow. Harding stood over Vikki and toed her lightly on the shoulder. When she moaned, he bent and picked up her rifle. Rummaging for McGriffin's rifle, he cradled both weapons and looked down at her. "You'd be better off with your boyfriend, bitch." He swung a rifle down and pointed it at her.

Hesitating, he dropped the weapon. "Dying's the easy way out. So much for your idealism. You didn't have a clue about Do'brai, or why I really wanted to do this, did you? Just be sure to let them know if they find you what this was really about." He turned for the plane.

McGriffin closed his eyes. Opening them, he watched Harding disappear into the night. He could get the rifle from Vikki, try and stop the airplane. He waited and made sure no one was watching him. He was about to move when a loud whining broke through the stillness: *an APU!* The auxiliary power unit ran up through the decibels. One of the C-130's engines coughed, then sputtered as it revved up. A second engine caught, and the meadow vibrated with the roar from the propellers.

McGriffin crouched and took an unsteady step forward. He tried to ignore the pain in his arm, but couldn't concentrate. He pulled a handkerchief from his pocket with his left hand and tried to wrap it around the wound. Fumbling at the cloth, he grew frustrated when he couldn't tie it, so he threw the handkerchief away.

The C-130 revved up engine three and started moving up the meadow. McGriffin shot a glance at Vikki. His eyes widened. *She's gone!* Wildly looking around, he couldn't see her. She must have dragged herself away. As the airplane moved out, he felt suddenly chilled. He had to do something.

There was nothing left to shoot with. He thought briefly about throwing rocks, but quickly shoved the idea away. His breathing quickened. *Christ alive, help me!* He spotted the HH-53 that Harding had abandoned. *Maybe they left something in there—anything.*

Keeping pressure on his right shoulder, he stumbled toward the helicopter. The grass whipped past, hindering his motion. The C-130 started slowing as it reached the top of the meadow. The landing lights were off. The pilot relied only on the starlight to guide him.

Staggering across the field, McGriffin reached the helicopter just as the 130 turned. He swung a foot up and pulled himself in with his good hand. He looked wildly around. Nothing. The C-130 thundered, bringing its fourth engine up. The helicopter vibrated from the sound. Channeled by the ring of mountain peaks, the plane threw its noise straight down the meadow.

Now think, he thought. What would a chopper pilot use in an emergency? They sit alert, but not for fighting—these things rescue people, they don't kill them. Come on, think!

Rescue! What would rescue use? Manny had said they were only used to rescue . . .

Flares!

He crawled to the front. Wincing in pain, McGriffin tore into several bags stenciled with undecipherable black lettering. He hauled out a flare gun. Steadying himself for a moment, he caught his breath. His arm felt as if it would fall off. He grasped the flare gun with his right hand, keeping his left plastered to his right shoulder.

Turning, he moved to the door and stumbled out. He dragged himself away from the helicopter and toward the center of the field. The C-130 ran up its engines, brakes creaking as if it were a racehorse straining against the starting gate.

The noise was overwhelming. He raised the flare gun, aiming for the cockpit. He'd have to wait until it was closer. If he were lucky, he might be able to distract the pilot. If not, he might bring attention to any aircraft searching for them—

"Drop it, Bill!" coughed Vikki.

McGriffin rotated his body. Vikki was on the ground, holding an M-16 on him. *She had the rifle Harding threw at her!* If he could get it—

"Vikki—"

"Drop it!" she shrilled.

McGriffin wet his lips. "Vikki, my God—the people that could die—"

"Think of the people that will *live*. The peace, the way people will have to change once they find out how *easy* it is to steal these weapons. Think of the groundswell it will cause." McGriffin took a step forward. "No closer." She coughed, then spat blood off to the side.

McGriffin tried to switch gears. He ignored the pounding in his shoulder. "Vikki, how could you do this—Harding tried to kill you. I can stop him—"

She twisted her mouth. Sitting on the ground, she looked up at him, holding her rifle steady. "You don't understand, do you? It's not him; it's not Anthony at all. It's what he can do if he succeeds. It's something we've dreamed about for years."

A tremendous roar washed over them. Turning, McGriffin saw the C-130 start moving. Slowly, it lumbered down the meadow, kicking up dust and grit in its prop wash. McGriffin turned back to Vikki. His eyes pleaded with her.

She raised her voice over the racket. "Drop it—"

McGriffin gritted his teeth and dove for the ground. Vikki's M-16 went off, spraying bullets over his head. The impulse knocked her backward. McGriffin brought the flare gun up. His hands wavering, he let off a charge, aiming over Vikki's head.

The night exploded in a mishmash of purple-green splotches. Vikki screamed and clutched at her eyes.

Rolling to his back, McGriffin let off a succession of three charges. He could barely see the plane. The fireballs burst into the night just as the C-130 rotated from the ground. One went off in front of the cockpit. Pushing himself up, he squinted to see the C-130 still airborne. Burning flesh and hair stung his nostrils.

As he watched, the 130's right wing dipped. Catching a tree at the end of the meadow, the aircraft spun around in slow motion. An explosion lit up the night. McGriffin could barely see through the spots before his eyes. The squat transport hit water and broke into pieces, skimming the surface. It burst into flames.

The fire flashed over the aircraft and spread to the meadow. The thought of the fire surrounding Vikki and him made him vomit. As he struggled up to stomp out the flames, he passed out.

23

"Don't move, Major. You've got an IV in you."

McGriffin opened his eyes. The ceiling jiggled crazily, like someone was bouncing the room up and down. JP-4 and antiseptic mixed in a bizarre potpourri of smells. The whooshing and movement brought him back to reality: he was inside a helicopter. He tried to move his hands but couldn't. They were bound to his sides.

His shoulder didn't hurt. It struck him that *nothing* hurt. Trying to move his arm again, he realized that he couldn't feel it. He opened his mouth—it felt cottony.

The nurse put a finger to his lips and smiled, shaking her head. "You're burned pretty badly, sir. We've got you doped up and will be air evacking you to Salt Lake City as soon as we reach Wendover."

233

"Man—Manny?" He was surprised at the sound of his voice. The words croaked out.

The nurse sternly admonished him. "No talking, Major."

"Howdy, sir." Chief Zolley pushed his face over McGriffin's. Zolley threw a look at the nurse. "I'll fill him in, Lieutenant. He's probably dying to know what's going on."

The nurse grimaced at his choice of words but moved back, allowing Chief Zolley to hunch forward.

"Captain Yarnez is right behind you. You're both going to be spending some time in the Shriner's burn unit. It took a while, but once the fires showed up on satellite, we were able to airlift nearly half the base to the mountains." He leaned closer. "You got them, Major. The DOE team recovered every stolen nuke. They weren't even scratched in those containers. You really did a Sierra Hotel job."

McGriffin tried to wet his lips. "Alf—Alf . . ."

"Alpha Base? It's surrounded with the rest of the security police force, plus some Marines flown in from Pendleton on Transatmospheric Vehicles. They rounded up the terrorists, including four in a Bronco, trying to get off base. No civilian air traffic is allowed anywhere near Wendover." He laughed. "There's some crazy first lieutenant, a big black security policeman, who was inside Alpha Base during the raid—he nearly took out the whole NEST and Broken Arrow teams when they didn't produce their ID's fast enough. He's acting like he's possessed." Zolley shook his head. "Between him and those two drunk fighter pilots—after the smoke cleared, we couldn't drag those two F-16 jocks out of the O'Club bar."

Moving his weight from one foot to the other, Zolley continued, "We were holed up in the command post for nearly two hours, trying to dig out from the explosions. Whoever planned that assault didn't have to do anything fancy: take out the centralized communications points and hit us when we were asleep." He grew somber. "They've got the girl under constant surveillance. She said something about Do'brai backing them before she passed out. Rumor is the administration isn't going to let them get away with it if it's true—something about a 'swift, decisive response.'

"Anyway, you missed the excitement at command post, but I'm sure the hell glad you weren't there. We would have never stopped them."

As the nurse approached, Chief Zolley clammed up.

"Sergeant, Major McGriffin needs his rest."

"Yes, ma'am." He stood and directed his comments to McGriffin. "I'm only along as an official observer from command post—Colonel DeVries wants an up-to-the-minute report on everything that happens." He grinned broadly. "He was ready to court-martial you when he discovered you left your post—but from all I've been hearing, you'll get an audience with the commander-in-chief after you're healed."

"Sergeant!"

Chief Zolley placed a hand on McGriffin's chest. "Good luck, sir." Zolley winked, then turned and nodded to the nurse before stepping to the rear.

The young lieutenant stuck a needle into the IV sac. "This will help you get back to sleep, Major. Just relax."

McGriffin blinked. Just relax, he thought dreamily. It wasn't like his problems were over. *Felowmate, Manny* . . . It felt great to be part of a team. It was the only thing in the world that could compare with flying, getting to work with guys like that. Like someone once said, "No matter how dark things get, that sun is always going to rise in the morning."

And then he thought of Vikki.

He steeled himself.

Maybe that sun wasn't going to rise after all, at least not for her. Funny how he thought he knew her. He wondered how much more he didn't know about her.

After this raid security at Alpha Base could only tighten, making it impossible for something like this to ever happen again. In a way, maybe Vikki got what she wanted after all.

As he drifted off to sleep, he felt placid. It wasn't like he'd ever get bored in the Air Force, even pulling a desk job.

Who'd have ever thought he'd see more excitement than flying?

THE BRILLIANT
NEW NOVEL BY
HAROLD COYLE
AUTHOR OF
SWORDPOINT

BRIGHT STAR

A boldly conceived Soviet attack threatens to overturn the balance of power in the Mediterranean—and bring the U.S. and the U.S.S.R. to open war.

Coming in March from Pocket Books!

40-01

POCKET
B O O K S

Printed in the United States
By Bookmasters